"Shh," Clay whispered.

Faced with the promise of tears, not knowing what else to do to calm her fears, Clay did what came naturally. He took Ilene into his arms and held her against him. She struggled for a second before giving in and letting him hold her.

A flood of feelings instantly rushed over him. Six years ago, he'd held her to him because they were wildly, unreasonably in love. Back then, he'd found himself loving—and being terrified of—the moment because she was in it.

She'd always had a special kind of power over him—until he'd taken it away from her. But now she needed comfort, and he needed to be able to give it to her.

Stroking her hair, he murmured against it, "It's going to be okay."

Dear Reader,

This year may be winding down, but the excitement's as high as ever here at Silhouette Intimate Moments. National bestselling author Merline Lovelace starts the month off with a bang with *A Question of Intent,* the first of a wonderful new miniseries called TO PROTECT AND DEFEND. Look for the next book, *Full Throttle,* in Silhouette Desire in January 2004.

Because you've told us you like miniseries, we've got three more for you this month. Marie Ferrarella continues her family-based CAVANAUGH JUSTICE miniseries with *Crime and Passion.* Then we have two military options: *Strategic Engagement* features another of Catherine Mann's WINGMEN WARRIORS, while Ingrid Weaver shows she can *Aim for the Heart* with her newest EAGLE SQUADRON tale. We've got a couple of superb stand-alone novels for you, too: *Midnight Run,* in which a wrongly accused cop has only one option— the heroine!—to save his freedom, by reader favorite Linda Castillo, and Laura Gale's deeply moving debut, *The Tie That Binds,* about a reunited couple's fight to save their daughter's life.

Enjoy them all—and we'll see you again next month, for six more of the best and most exciting romances around.

Yours,

Leslie J. Wainger
Executive Editor

Please address questions and book requests to:
Silhouette Reader Service
U.S.: 3010 Walden Ave., P.O. Box 1325, Buffalo, NY 14269
Canadian: P.O. Box 609, Fort Erie, Ont. L2A 5X3

Crime and Passion
MARIE FERRARELLA

Published by Silhouette Books

America's Publisher of Contemporary Romance

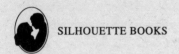 **SILHOUETTE BOOKS**

ISBN 0-373-27326-6

CRIME AND PASSION

Copyright © 2003 by Marie Rydzynski-Ferrarella

Printed in U.S.A.

Books by Marie Ferrarella in Miniseries

MARIE FERRARELLA

writes books distinguished by humor and natural dialogue. This RITA® Award-winning author's goal is to make people laugh and feel good. She has written over one hundred books for Silhouette, some under the name Marie Nicole. Her romances are beloved by fans worldwide.

To
Brett Walker Richman.
Welcome to the world.

Chapter 1

Whistle-blower.

Ilene O'Hara frowned as she looked at the front cover of the magazine she'd just unearthed from beneath the tangled mass of toys in Alex's toy box. Her five-year-old must have accidentally tossed the magazine into the box during one of the few times she'd gotten him to actually pick up after himself.

After taking it out, she leaned against the wall, sat crossed-legged on the floor and stared at the magazine. The cover depicted three bold, confident-looking women, all of whom had been instrumental in stirring up intense investigations into three separate institutions once thought of as towers of respectability and bastions of power.

When she'd originally bought the magazine, she'd

never thought that someday she might be considering joining the ranks of an elite group of people nicknamed, not with complete fondness, whistle-blowers. Nobody really liked whistle-blowers, no matter how necessary those people might be for the well-being of the economy or society in general. To the firm on which they were blowing the whistle, they were deemed traitors. In truth, the public probably wasn't too crazy about them, either.

Wasn't that the edict of the playground? Nobody liked a tattletale?

With a sigh Ilene got up and tossed the magazine onto the coffee table before picking up the last armload of toys and bringing them to rest within the toy box. Upstairs, Alex was asleep, worn-out by a long day of play.

Ilene was worn-out as well, but playing had nothing to do with it. Wrestling with your conscience took a lot out of you.

She looked around, a restlessness chewing holes in her usual boundless energy. The rest of the room could wait until tomorrow. Surrendering, Ilene sank down on the tan sofa, her mind once again locked in a silent, one-woman debate over whether or not she should do what she knew in her heart was the right thing. But no one had died and left her the mantle of martyr, she insisted.

Inactivity seemed so seductive right now. Maybe she would just keep her mouth shut. Would it really be so bad to close her eyes and continue as if nothing were wrong? As if things were not out of sync? As if the corporation wasn't playing hide-and-seek with a huge amount of money?

She didn't feel she was on some kind of sacred mission here. Her parents hadn't exactly given her much of a moral foundation from which to build.

She glanced at the one photograph she had of her parents that hung on the far wall. It was a studio shot, and they'd been forced to smile. She didn't ever remember them smiling. Not on their own. They'd always been too busy sniping at each other and being covertly resentful of the daughter who had been the reason they had—in an unguarded moment of guilt—joined together legally and wound up wasting what were supposed to be "the good years."

They'd stay married until neither one could stand the other. Until she was eighteen. Try as she might, Ilene couldn't remember one drop of love being spilt in that house.

Nonetheless, Ilene had always had a strong sense of right and wrong. Even if she hadn't, it didn't take a would-be saint to know that misleading stockholders, a vast amount of stockholders, was wrong.

Especially if it was being done on purpose.

And since John Walken, her boss and the vice president in charge of the audit department of Simplicity Computers—one of the leading computer companies of the country, if not *the* leading company—hadn't gotten back to her on the audit figures she'd uncovered more than a week ago, she knew the so-called discrepancy was not accidental. She had secretly hoped it would be.

After she'd brought him the news, she'd watched the handsome man pale ever so slightly beneath his perfect Maui tan before he'd flashed a brilliant, engaging smile and told her not to worry, that he'd take care of matters.

He'd all but patted her on her head as he'd ushered her out of his tastefully decorated office with its fifty-inch plasma TV on one wall. He thanked her for her keen diligence and promised her a bonus for what amounted to doing her job. Less than an hour later, he'd sent one of his assistants to press two tickets to Los Angeles into her hand, along with complimentary passes to Disneyland. Walken had expressed in the enclosed note that he had heard about her wanting to take her son there someday. The man made it a point to know his people, one of the things she'd always liked about him. Now she wondered if he just wanted to know which buttons to press when dealing with a subordinate in a challenging situation.

She'd been too stunned to speak at first, then politely had returned the tickets, saying that with the holidays coming up, this was an inconvenient time of the year to travel. It wasn't strictly true. There was no one she spent the holidays with outside of Alex. She didn't know where her parents were and there were no siblings, no aunts or uncles to populate her life. She and Alex could have picked up at any time and gone.

But the offer of the tickets hadn't sat right with her. Neither had the discrepancy, even though she'd wanted to believe in Walken, to believe in the company to which she'd given almost four years of her life. Initially she'd clung to the hope of a plausible explanation as to why the expenses slated for Simplicity's ledgers had been ascribed to one of their holding companies instead, sending that small company to the brink of bankruptcy. She passionately refused to believe that she'd made yet another mistake in placing her faith with the wrong recipient.

Just as she had with Clay.

Ilene could feel her eyes stinging and closed them defensively.

No.

She wasn't going to go there. That was a place that she'd deliberately walled up even before Alex was born, but most definitely afterward. Loving Clay, believing in Clay might have been a mistake, but doing so had led her to the greatest joy of her life. It had given her Alex.

She could have reached the greatest of heights careerwise, but without Alex in her life, nothing else would have mattered. She was meant to be a mother first and foremost, and everything else second. Every fiber in her being told her so. There was a vast amount of love within her, love that had been thwarted by her parents, disregarded by Clay. But now it was all channeled toward Alex.

And it was because of Alex, she told herself, that she was going to have to blow the whistle.

There was no other path open to her. She never wanted to look into her son's eyes and see an accusation, or worse, disappointment shining there. And if she didn't bring the discrepancy she'd found to light, if she allowed Simplicity—a company that was well respected and touted as one of the few safe investments still left on the shaky stock market boards—to continue lying to the unsuspecting public, she wasn't going to be able to live with her conscience. Because when the truth finally came out, it would steal millions of dollars away from everyday people who could ill afford to have something like this happen to them.

Ilene dragged her hand through her long, strawberry-blond hair. She knew what she had to do. Right thing or not, she still couldn't help being afraid. But then, she supposed Joan of Arc had been afraid, too.

Pushing up from the sofa, Ilene rose to her feet. It was late and time to go to bed. Tomorrow she'd do what she had to do.

She tried not to dwell on the fact that Joan of Arc ended up being burned at the stake.

Almost holding her breath, Ilene sat perfectly still as the woman behind the desk studied her. Pert, blond, the woman hardly looked old enough to have graduated from college, much less law school…and much too young to have attained her present position of assistant district attorney. She looked as if she would have been more at home being interviewed for Rose Bowl Queen than taking part in a criminal court hearing.

Ilene glanced down at the woman's name plate. Janelle Cavanaugh.

The name Cavanaugh leaped out at her.

Was it a coincidence? Or was this just fate's lopsided sense of humor aiming itself right between her eyes? Ilene tried to regain control over herself. It wasn't as if Cavanaugh was an uncommon name, she argued. But here in Aurora, most of the Cavanaughs who were related to Clay were in some sort of law enforcement.

As was he, she'd heard. Those had been his plans when they'd gone together. He was one of those types who always got what he was after. He just hadn't been after her.

Janelle Cavanaugh folded her hands before her, seemingly calm in the face of the bombshell that had been placed on her desk. Her eyes never left Ilene's. "You have proof?"

Ilene met her gaze. "I wouldn't be wasting your time if I didn't."

It amazed Ilene that her hands were so still. Inside, she was shaking like a leaf as she reached into her briefcase and took out the printed copies of the files she had audited. The originals were still safely in their place and gave no indication that once she'd stumbled across one discrepancy, she'd conducted an internal audit of her own. Ilene had discovered the tip of the iceberg when it came to corporate corruption. The discrepancy was huge between the true figures and the ones the board was about to release to stockholders in its annual disclosure.

The world at large believed that Simplicity had had a banner year. In truth, the profits were false. A mountain of expenditures had been hidden from the shareholders, making Simplicity seem as if ownership in the company was a very desirable thing in a troubled fiscal age.

She understood the thinking behind the ruse, or thought she did. If investors flocked to Simplicity, waving their money before them, Simplicity would eventually collect enough money to cover their debts and yield at least part of the profit it reported. But if something were to happen, if a story should be leaked to the business world, confidence and stock would plummet and many people would be bankrupt, their accounts completely wiped out.

She knew she couldn't live with that on her conscience. That was why she was here. This problem had to be cleared up before it went any further.

Janelle quickly scanned the top pages she'd taken out of the manila envelope. Sporting the expressionless face her brothers and cousins swore made her so perfect for playing poker, she raised her eyes to the delicate-looking woman before her.

From all appearances Ilene O'Hara looked as if she belonged on the fast track at some pricey modeling agency. Tall, slender, she had a regal composure and a face that begged for magazine covers. Janelle supposed that was what her cousin had seen in the woman in the first place.

Janelle doubted that Ilene O'Hara even remembered that they had met once, although fleetingly. Six years ago, she thought, give or take a little. She'd stumbled across Clay and his girlfriend of the moment at a coffee shop. Clay had looked a little uncomfortable making introductions, and she'd known it was because he hated being pinned down. Janelle remembered thinking that Clay had finally found someone who didn't look as if she was living just to have a good time.

But then Clay and Ilene had broken up. He'd been a little funny for a while. Always gregarious, he'd become withdrawn. No one in the family had guessed why. She'd been the only one who even knew about Ilene. In time, he'd bounced back to his old self. But Janelle had felt that the girl had left a permanent impression.

She smiled warmly now at Ilene. "So, how have you been?"

Ilene blinked. The A.D.A. was making polite chit-chat. Why? "Excuse me?"

Janelle's smile widened. "You don't remember

me, do you?'' Small wonder—Ilene had been very wrapped up with her cousin then.

Ilene glanced at the name plate again before raising her eyes back to Janelle. She began to look familiar. ''Then you are related to Clay.''

''Guilty as charged.'' She leaned into Ilene, allowing herself one more private moment, in part to make the woman less uncomfortable about being here. ''I always thought he was a jerk for walking away from you.''

It wasn't what Ilene wanted to discuss. Not now. Not ever. ''He was too young. We were too young,'' Ilene amended. She shifted in the seat, gripping the arms, eager, now that she had started the ball rolling, to get on with it. ''So where do we go from here?''

There were a myriad of details to be faced. However, Janelle had her own set of priorities that differed slightly from those of the D.A.'s office. ''First thing we do is get you police protection.''

Ilene's eyes widened at the ominous pronouncement. Police protection was for people who feared for their lives. People who were in danger. That wasn't her. She knew all the people in her department. They were people with whom she'd attended Christmas parties, people whose birthdays she'd celebrated. None of them would hurt her. Despite its size, the company had a reputation as being one big, happy family.

And she'd never been one who'd ever meekly

obeyed without question. "Police protection? Why? This isn't The Mob we're dealing with."

"No," Janelle agreed, "these are CEOs with a great deal to lose. People facing exposure do desperate things." Janelle could tell that Ilene didn't like what she was hearing. "Welcome to the twenty-first century." She got down to business. "Does anyone know you've come here?"

Ilene shook her head. She'd taken a personal day, telling the office she was going to the doctor. She'd told Alex's baby-sitter the same thing. Coming here wasn't something she enjoyed advertising. "No."

Janelle tried to read between the lines. "But you did go to your boss about this?"

Ilene could tell by the other woman's tone that she thought Ilene had made a tactical mistake. But Janelle Cavanaugh didn't know John Walken, didn't know that he was an honorable man.

"Yes," her own tone was defensive, "I thought he'd want to fix it, that he didn't know this was going on. I can't find out who gave the initial order."

Janelle looked at her knowingly. "And Walken said he would get right on it, but you haven't heard anything so far."

Ilene hated the way this all sounded so predictable. There had to be some explanation. Good people didn't do heinous things.

But if she truly believed that, why was she here?

She looked down at her nails, rendering the

answer through teeth that were almost closed. "Right."

Janelle nodded. "And how long ago was that?"

"A week." It sounded like an eternity. "I thought about talking to him again." Ilene had almost gone in today, wanting to give Walken another chance. She'd changed her mind at the last minute. "But—"

"Your instincts told you to come here." Janelle's blue eyes smiled at the other woman. "Good instincts. Hope your survival ones are just as keen."

"Is this police-protection thing really necessary?"

"It is if I want to sleep at night. Excuse me for a second." Janelle drew the phone in closer to her.

Turning her body away from her, Janelle let her fingers quickly tap out the familiar numbers. Her father, Brian, was the current chief of detectives and the younger of the two surviving Cavanaugh brothers. His three sons, her brothers and six of her seven cousins were also with the police force. Only Patience had broken free, following her own destiny to become a veterinarian. But even Patience had continuing contact with the police force. Janelle's cousin treated the German shepherds that made up the K-9 squad.

There were times when Janelle thought of the police force as her personal cavalry. This was one of those times.

Connected to her father's private line, she lowered her voice as she began to speak. After a few moments of obligatory give and take and a promise to stop by "soon," Janelle told her father why she was calling. Quickly, she gave him Ilene's background story and what she'd brought to the table.

Listening to her father's answer, Janelle had no way of knowing she was setting into motion something that was going to mushroom out until it touched all of them.

"You look much too happy for a Monday morning," Kyle Santini, Clay's partner of two years grumbled as he slumped down in his own seat. The sudden action all but sent his coffee sloshing over the sides of the chipped, worn mug his five-year-old had made him in camp last year. Carefully, he set the misshapen royal-blue mug on his desk, keeping it away from any important papers. Kyle eyed the man considered by the squad to be the personification of the carefree, happy bachelor. "You still seeing that stripper?"

"Exotic dancer," Clay corrected. "And no, I'm not still seeing her. Ginger and I came to a parting of the ways more than a week ago."

A knowing look came over Santini's face. "Let me guess, she wanted to have 'the talk.'" Taking a long drag of the mud that passed for coffee in the precinct, Kyle chuckled to himself. "Sooner or later, they all want to have 'the talk.'" Kyle shook his head, a man to whom women would always remain a mystery. "What is it about women that makes them want to clip a man's wings?"

"I don't know," Clay said honestly. "But it never got that far with Ginger and me."

He thought of the woman he'd seen a handful of times in the past six weeks. One fateful night her screams had brought him into the alley where she'd been dragged by some low life intent on turning his fantasy into reality. Rescuing her had earned him Ginger's gratitude and a few other things, as well. The woman had a body that wouldn't quit and a mind that wouldn't start.

Even though he'd told himself that was exactly what he wanted at this stage of his life, Clay had found himself getting restless and looking for an excuse to end the romance. The woman had given him one when she'd suggested a threesome.

"Ginger was a free spirit," he told a more than mildly interested Santini. "She just wanted to be a little freer than I liked."

Kyle groaned as if he'd just been deprived of his reason for living. "Don't let my mind go there. You're talking to a monk."

Clay grinned. In the past six weeks, this had been a familiar complaint. "Alice is just about due, isn't she?"

"If you ask me, she's about overdue." Santini sighed. Apparently prenatal was no better than postnatal. "Then I get to listen to her complain about how men should be the ones to have the kids."

Shaking his head, Kyle shot Clay an envious look. "You don't know how lucky you are, being a bachelor."

"Yeah, lucky," Clay echoed then laughed. His partner wasn't fooling anyone. He'd cut off his right arm before he'd give up what he had. "I've seen you with your son. You wouldn't change that for the world."

"No, but there are times I'd be willing to trade Alice in, at least for a weekend."

Clay rocked back in his chair. He knew better. "Any man looks at her twice, you're ready to knock them into last year."

Santini shrugged. "That's beside the point. That's just my hot temper."

Straightening up, Clay decided these reports weren't going to file themselves, no matter how much he wished they would. He got busy, or tried to. "Nothing wrong in admitting you love the woman you married, Santini. Not enough of that going around."

Santini clearly wasn't interested in platitudes, he was interested in details. Preferably juicy ones. "You still didn't answer me. If you didn't get a little last night, why are you grinning like some loony hyena?"

Clay knew his answer was going to disappoint the man. "Because I just found out we're going to have a judge in the family. My sister's getting married."

"You're going to give me more of a hint than

that, Cavanaugh. You've got three sisters," Santini reminded him.

"Callie."

Clay couldn't remember his older sister ever looking so excited. She'd waited until they'd all sat down to Sunday dinner. For once, his father had managed to corral everyone, even his uncle. They'd all but poured out of the dining room, even with the extra leaves added on to the table his dad had specially made for family affairs.

Putting two fingers into her mouth, Callie had whistled the way she used to as a kid, getting the roar at the table to die down to a whisper and then, as sweet as could be, she'd made the announcement. She and Brent were getting married. And just like that, he was going to become an uncle, thanks to the judge's five-year-old daughter, Rachel.

"You're kidding me." Santini whistled, shaking his head. "Damn, and here I was hoping she'd give me a tumble after I leave Alice."

"Fat chance. In more ways than one." Clay paused. "Why don't you call up and send your wife flowers?"

Kyle laughed. Flowers were usually to apologize for something. "That'll throw her." And then he grinned. "Maybe I will."

Captain Reynolds leaned into the cubicle, his gray eyes sweeping over both the men. "Cavanaugh, Santini, the chief just called. He wants the two of you to protect a witness. Apparently this is a big deal. The D.A. doesn't want anything to happen to her.''

Clay rolled his eyes. He'd never been much for baby-sitting detail. One of the desk jockeys could do just as well. ''I've got a desk full of work.''

The gray-haired man looked at him, his manner friendly but brooking no nonsense. Reynolds liked to stay on top of things at all times, which meant exercising control, but never holding the leash too tight. Taut leashes had a way of snapping.

''Which'll still be there whether or not you pull this detail. Consider it a vacation with pay.'' About to withdraw, Reynolds stopped again. ''Either of you boys got any stock in Simplicity Computers, I suggest you cash it in right now. Seems one of the internal auditors found some dirty business going on.''

Clay sighed. Terrific. A whistle-blower. ''This have something to do with the person we're supposed to be guarding?''

Reynolds nodded. ''It does.''

''This person have a name?''

''Yeah.'' Reynolds paused to think a moment. ''Ilene O'Hara.''

Feeling like someone who had just slipped into the Twilight Zone without so much as a warning flash of light, Clay stared at the captain.

The smile had vanished from Clay's lips.

Chapter 2

All during the ride to the D.A.'s office Clay had been silently steeling himself for the ordeal ahead.

Beside him, in the driver's seat, Santini sat expounding on whatever topic floated through his dark head. Occasionally coming up for air, his partner's nonstop flow of words only managed to bounce off Clay's ears, hardly penetrating as he thought about the woman he was going to be seeing after all this time.

Ilene O'Hara.

It had been six years. Six years and three months, but who was counting, he thought with a self-deprecating smile. He and Ilene had broken up in August and now they were looking down the calendar at November. Technically, she had broken up with him, but he'd driven her to it. On purpose.

Ilene O'Hara.

He'd thought she'd left Aurora. When had she gotten back? Clay glanced out the window, barely seeing the scenery go by as Santini took the streets a little quicker than they were meant to be taken.

Clay didn't know how he felt about seeing her again. He was trying not to feel anything at all, but that wasn't working out too well. Emotions insisted on rumbling through him. He was like a channel surfer who'd accidentally come across an episode of a program he'd once enjoyed. There was a sense of familiarity washing over him, perhaps even a vague sense of nostalgia, but nothing more.

He couldn't let there be anything more.

"Where the hell are you today?" Santini's voice finally elbowed its way into his thoughts, demanding his attention. Demanding a response.

Turning, Clay looked at him. "What?"

"You," Santini repeated impatiently, turning a corner and going down the street that would eventually lead them to the D.A.'s office. "Where are you?"

Clay stopped himself from bracing his hand against the dashboard. "Here, next to you, risking my life as you take turns too fast and give all detectives a bad name."

Santini snorted. "Don't give me that. First you come in looking as if you'd been peeled off the top of the morning, now you look like the used gum that you peel off the bottom of someone's heel."

Santini spared him a penetrating glance before looking back on the road. "After riding around with you
for two years, I know that you're not one of those
sensitive guys, so this isn't a mood swing. What
gives?"

Santini was his partner, and he shared as much
with him as he shared with any man or any member
of his family. At times even more. But right now he
didn't feel like talking about it. He didn't even want
to let his thoughts stray in that direction. He just
wanted the assignment to be magically over instead
of just beginning.

"Just drive."

Santini mumbled something unintelligible under
his breath, but Clay managed to pick up enough of
it to know that the man was casting aspersions on
closed-mouth black Irishmen. For the first time since
he'd heard Ilene's name this morning, Clay smiled.

She looked better than he'd expected.

Six years had taken the promise of beauty and
had lovingly polished it until it shone. She'd
changed, he realized. She didn't look innocent anymore. Just knowledgeable, as if she now knew that
the world wasn't some huge playground with all the
safety features built into it.

He supposed that was partially his fault. If he
hadn't pushed her toward it, maybe they wouldn't
have broken up.

Maybe…

The land of maybe was mist-filled territory with long, winding, intersecting roads that led nowhere, and Clay wasn't about to go there. Today was what it was and so was he, there was no point in speculating otherwise. Ultimately he knew he wouldn't have been any good for her. A woman like Ilene needed stability, and stability scared the hell out of him.

Stability and stagnation both began with the same letter.

As he walked into the room, Clay glanced down at her left hand. She was wearing a ring on the appropriate finger, but it wasn't a wedding ring. It was sporting a blue stone in its center.

Her birthstone was blue. Sapphire, he thought, not aquamarine. Funny the things you remembered even after all this time.

Her profile had been toward him. When she turned around to look at him, he saw her mouth drop open a second before she shut it again. She was absolutely stunned. He'd always loved the way surprise had blossomed on her face. But this wasn't that kind of surprise. This was more like shock. She hadn't known he was the one being called in.

Clay's eyes shifted toward his cousin Janelle, the only other person in the small, book-lined room besides his partner who had just entered.

So that was it. Janelle.

He might have known.

This was her idea, he was sure of it, even though

the order had come down to him from Captain
Reynolds. Janelle fancied herself a puppeteer, or-
chestrating the lives of those around her. He'd figured himself immune. Obviously, he'd figured
wrong.

They were going to have to have a talk, he and
Janelle. She meddled in things that didn't concern
her, more even, than his sisters did.

As blameless as Mother Teresa, Janelle was on
her feet in a moment, rounding her desk and coming
to greet her cousin and his partner. She nodded at
the latter while flashing a broad, encouraging and
amazingly guileless smile at Clay.

"Thanks for coming so quickly. Ms. O'Hara, this
is Detective Kyle Santini." The pause was almost
imperceptible as she added, "And you already know
my cousin."

"Yes." Normally a warm, outgoing person, Ilene
could feel herself withdrawing. Freezing up. "I
know your cousin."

Her eyes, Ilene hoped, were cool as she regarded
Clay. Her voice and expression were about all she
felt she could control. As for her heart, well, that
had launched into double time, beating as if she
were free-falling off the edge of a cliff. God knows
she hadn't expected this.

She took a small breath to steady herself before
asking, with what she prayed was slight disinterest,
"How have you been?"

Clay felt as if he needed an ice pick just to chip

out the words she'd directed his way. They were two strangers, unceremoniously pushed together on the dance floor. And neither one of them wanted to dance.

"I'm doing all right," he replied. His eyes shifted toward Janelle. "Captain Reynolds got a call saying something about a witness needing protection?" The words hung in the air like a challenge.

He was mad, Ilene thought, and she didn't know why. Men were so damn hard to figure out at times.

"That was my idea," Janelle acknowledged.

Clay's blue eyes were steely as they regarded his cousin. "I'm sure it was."

"But it's not mine," Ilene declared. This was an omen. She shouldn't have come.

Rising to her feet, struggling not to hurry from the room or say anything that would give away the shaky state of her emotions, Ilene tightened her hand around the purse strap hanging from her shoulder. The air supply in the small room decreased at an alarming rate. She needed to get out of here. Now.

She'd left Aurora for a while. When she'd returned, she'd always known she'd run into him someday. Aurora wasn't small, but even in cities like San Francisco and L.A., paths sometimes crossed unwillingly and Aurora was smaller than either of those places.

Even so, she'd hoped that when the day did come, she'd be prepared, that some hidden sixth sense would have forewarned her before she was suddenly thrust into his presence. Then at least she would have felt confident enough to put on a decent performance. One that would convince him that he hadn't broken her heart in a million pieces.

But right now she had her son and her work and that was more than enough.

Except that now she didn't have her work, Ilene reminded herself. Or possibly a future, either. She struggled against sinking into a pool of emotional quicksand.

Her hands tightened around her strap again as she deliberately addressed her words to the dark-haired man behind Clay. "Look, I'm sorry you were called out for nothing, but I've changed my mind."

"I'm afraid you can't do that," Janelle protested.

Ilene looked at the other woman. She'd never been able to tolerate restrictions well. "Watch me." But as she began to leave the room, it was Clay, not Janelle, who got in her way.

He was a cop first, he reminded himself. And the situation needed one. "Captain Reynolds doesn't throw around the term 'protection' lightly. Now what's this about?"

"Ms. O'Hara says that her boss is misrepresenting her company's profits to the public," Janelle said.

Her company.

It occurred to Clay that he didn't even know where Ilene worked or what she even did for a living. They'd been involved while in college, when everything was promising and fresh, and paths hadn't been laid down yet. He'd always felt she could be anything she wanted to be. After they'd split and she'd left town, he'd purposely tried not to keep tabs on her, knowing if he did, he might be tempted to do something stupid, like tell her what a fool he'd been to walk away from her.

He would have hurt her if he'd remained. He knew that just as surely as he knew his own name. But men like him didn't marry, Clay reminded himself. They dallied and went on. His one true love was the force and always would be.

"You work for Simplicity Computers, right?" he heard Santini inquiring.

"Yes, I do," Ilene replied tersely.

At least until they find out what I've done. And then she wouldn't be working for anyone. There was money in the bank, but that would only last a little while. How was she going to provide for Alex then? *Oh God, this was a huge mistake.*

Santini gave a low whistle. "You're kidding. I just bought one of those starter computers for my kid."

"It's not going to self-destruct," Ilene told him, her eyes covertly shifting to Clay. Trying not to see how time had only made him better looking. "The problem isn't with the product quality. It's still the finest that money can buy," she assured Santini. "That's the problem."

"How do you mean?" Clay asked.

"A great deal of money has gone into producing the best on the market and—" Ilene stopped abruptly. She couldn't think about that. She'd made a mistake. A bad one. It had taken seeing Clay again to make her come to her senses. She needed to retreat. "Never mind. I just want to go home." Wanting to flee, she reached for the folder she'd brought.

But Janelle picked it up, holding it to herself protectively. "You came here because you wanted to do the right thing. Don't let anything change your mind."

A civil war raged inside her. "All right," Ilene surrendered, but only partially. "Keep the folder. I'll be in touch."

"Ms. O'Hara, I meant what I said about your needing protection. Fortunes are at stake here. Careers, not to mention jail sentences," Janelle emphasized. "If your bosses suspect that you came here—"

"Then keep my name out of it," Ilene said.

"Just because they're busy trying to hoodwink the public doesn't mean they're oblivious to everything else," Janelle cautioned her. She glanced toward Clay as if to garner his support, but he was silent. "If you've already brought this to your boss's attention, he knows that you know and it won't take a rocket scientist to make the connection."

Ilene deliberately pushed the thought to the conclusion she thought the woman was trying to reach. "And when he does, he'll do what? Kill me?"

"Maybe," Clay interjected.

Ilene swung around. "He wouldn't do that," she insisted. "He coaches his son's Little League."

Clay laughed shortly. For all her worldly appearance, Ilene was apparently still naive. "Ever see how the parents can mix it up over an incorrect call?"

Ilene raised her chin in a way he was all too familiar with. It was part of her go-to-hell stance. He'd once found that adorable. Now he found it irritating.

"I'll be fine," she said tersely. "If I have police protection, *then* they might suspect something."

"How will they know unless they're staking out your place?" Clay posed.

The question stopped Ilene in her tracks for a second. She had no answer for that. No, they were trying to frighten her, she thought, trying to make sure she testified. Well, the files spoke for themselves, they didn't need her.

Squaring her shoulders, she moved to open the door. Clay wrapped his hand around her wrist, gently holding her in place. She looked up, startled. But instead of detaining her, he turned her hand over and placed a small white card into her palm. She looked at him quizzically.

"We can't force you to accept protection, but if anything goes wrong, call one of those numbers. The top one belongs to the precinct, the bottom one is my cell phone."

She tried to give the card back to him. "I won't be needing this."

But Clay raised his hands before him, unwilling to take the business card back. "You never know."

Her eyes met his for a long moment. "No," she said significantly, "you never do." And then she left the office.

Annoyed, frustrated and feeling a little as if a part of him had just been unceremoniously raked over hot coals, Clay shook his head.

"That has got to be the most stubborn woman I ever met. And considering present company," he looked pointedly at Janelle, "that's saying a hell of a lot. Do me a favor, Janelle, next time you have the urge to take out your bow and arrow and play Cupid—find another target."

"I'm sure I don't know what you're talking about. All I see is a woman who needs protecting. You're the best man for the job, that's all. You, too, Santini," she added, looking at the other man.

"Why do I get the feeling I'm an afterthought here?" Santini looked at his partner. "You and the lady have a history I should know about?"

"No," Clay said flatly. "If we're done here, A.D.A, my partner here and I'd like to get back to work."

Janelle spread her hands helplessly. "I'm afraid it looks like you're done. For now." She sat down behind her desk and began to go through the contents of the envelope again.

"Good. C'mon, Santini, let's go."

"You *do* have a history," Santini insisted as he followed his partner through the door. "C'mon, Cavanaugh, you're talking to a deprived man here. I'm withering on the vine. Give."

Clay had absolutely no intentions of satisfying the man's insatiable curiosity. "Shut up, Santini," he grumbled as he lengthened his stride toward the elevator.

It took Ilene the entire drive home to calm down, to get her hands to remain steady on the steering wheel. After all this time, Clay still had an effect on her. Could still make her pulse dance just by being in the same room as her.

Except that this time she had no illusions about him. He wasn't the Prince Charming she'd thought—that she'd hoped he'd be. Like the old song said, no man burning with a pure, radiant light in the night.

Besides, she argued with herself, she'd gotten swept away in the excitement of what she was proposing to do. It had clouded her thinking. Walken would never hurt her. The most he would do is fire her, and she certainly couldn't blame him for that. Not the way she blamed him for sweeping all those numbers under a proverbial rug, she thought grimly. She knew he was only thinking of saving the company, but she'd never believed that the end justified the means, not when the means involved fraud.

She was overthinking again.

God, but she needed some solace, a reprieve, if only for a little while, from the whole situation. She needed to do something fun, something carefree with Alex. There was a soul-renewing purity in her son's innocence, in the echo of his laugh, that always helped her get back on course. Even when loneliness threatened to drag her down to unmeasurable depths.

Making an impulsive decision, she called her baby sitter and asked her not to pick up Alex today. Then she went and sprang her son from his nursery school.

"Hi, Mama." He beamed at her. "Where are we going?"

"What makes you think we're going somewhere, sport?"

His eyes danced as he looked at her. "Because we always go someplace when you come."

"Can't pull the wool over your eyes, can I, Alex?" He cocked his head, looking at her. She could almost see him pulling in the words, trying to make sense of them. Sometimes she just wanted to eat him all up, he was that dear to her. "We're going to the park, Alex. That okay with you?"

Alex loved the park. If she let him, he'd be happy to live there. "Okay," he echoed, dragging her by the hand to the car.

And they were off.

She was so busy enjoying Alex, enjoying the day,

that she didn't become aware of the feeling until sometime into the second hour. The feeling that someone was watching her.

At first she convinced herself that the A.D.A., aided and abetted by Clay, had spooked her and that she only imagined things. After all, the park was full of parents, mainly mothers, with their children. With all that movement around her, it was easy enough to mistake that for someone watching her. The main park in Aurora had rides galore and diversions for children of all ages. At any given time, a great many people populated the area.

Despite her arguments to the contrary, the gnawing feeling that there was someone shadowing her persisted. Drawing her courage together, Ilene pretended to go the ladies' room with Alex. Once inside, the boy looked puzzled as they began to leave by the rear exit. "We playing a game, Mama?"

"Yes, a game, Alex. Kind of like hide-and-seek." Holding his hand, she circled around until she was behind the front entrance again.

She was doing it to prove to herself that she was imagining things.

She wasn't.

No wonder she felt as if she was being shadowed. She was. Clay was leaning against a tree, watching the entrance. Waiting for her to emerge again.

Angry, she grabbed him by the shoulder and pulled him around to face her. It was hard to keep from shouting at him, but she didn't want to frighten Alex. "Why are you following me?"

Clay looked at her, not surprised that she had caught on, only that she had done it so quickly. But one of the things he'd always liked about her was that she was sharper than any woman he'd ever been with.

"Because Janelle and Captain Reynolds seem to think you're in danger."

"The only thing I seem to be in danger of is running into people from my past who I don't want to see."

Though tempted to make a flippant reply, Clay was more interested in the small boy whose hand she held. The one looking up at him with big blue eyes and a thousand-watt smile so like his mother's.

He nodded at the boy. "Is this your son?"

Ilene placed her hands protectively on the boy's shoulders as he stood in front of her. "Yes, this is Alex."

Not standing on ceremony, Alex tugged on Clay's shirt and said, "Hi."

He spared the boy a smile in kind. "Hi." Clay raised his eyes to Ilene. The boy's existence raised a host of questions in his mind, questions he should have been able to bank down. "When did you get married?"

She felt her back stiffening. "That is none of your business and neither am I. Go away, Detective Cavanaugh. Before I call a cop."

He couldn't resist. "Half the force is related to me."

"Then I'll find someone who isn't," she said over her shoulder as she hurried away with her son.

This time Clay remained where he was.

Chapter 3

"Leaving already?"

On his way through the crowded bar where he and other members of the police department gathered at the end of a long, hard day, Clay stopped several feet short of his goal, the front door. Even with the din cranked up an extra decibel or two, he still recognized the familiar voice. He'd been hearing it for all of his twenty-seven years.

The bar was extra crowded tonight with retired as well as active police personnel taking up much of the available space. They'd come together to throw a party for one of their own. After several false starts at retirement, Detective Alvin "Willie-Boy" Jenkins was finally leaving the force. The older, florid-faced man had been a fixture with the department for as long as Clay could remember, having even gone six years partnered with his father until Andrew had been promoted to chief of police.

It was Andrew Cavanaugh who had cleared up the mystery behind Willie-Boy's nickname. It derived not from a familiar form of a name given him at birth, but from the fact that the police detective had become enamored with the old Robert Redford movie, *Tell Them Willie Boy Was Here.* He had seen it more times than even he could remember and could spout off lines of dialogue at the drop of a hat. No one knew why he was so fascinated with that particular piece of celluloid and no one wanted to ask. Willie-Boy tended to be very long-winded once he got started.

Clay had toyed with the idea of saying good-night to the members of his family who were still in attendance, then decided that slipping out unnoticed was the better way to go. He'd underestimated his father's eagle eye. At an age when most men were squinting to make out the written page or see beyond the reach of their hand, his father's vision was still twenty-twenty.

"Keeping tabs on me, Dad?" Clay turned to face the older man.

Andrew raised a mug of dark brew and took a small sip before answering. "No, just wondering what's up. You're usually one of the last to go."

Clay shrugged, looking away. "I'm starting a new trend."

The hell he was, Andrew thought.

Andrew wasn't one to pry into his children's affairs. Or so he liked to claim. In reality, the complete opposite was true. He took his role as father to heart and it had only intensified ever since his wife had disappeared fifteen years ago.

That was the way he saw it. Rose had disappeared. Which meant that someday she would reappear. He refused to accept the fact that she had walked out of his life with heated, hurtful words hanging in the air between them, and then died. Everyone else outside of the family had long since taken the scenario as a given. Rose Cavanaugh had died in the river where her car was discovered. But since neither her body nor her purse had ever been recovered, to Andrew the case was still open.

Rose was still his wife and she was out there somewhere, waiting to be found.

And Clay was still his son, one of two, and always would be no matter what his age. Being a father meant being concerned. Rose would have wanted it that way.

He studied his younger son closely now. His instincts, rather than mellow, had only grown sharper with age. "Something eating at you, Clay?"

Yes, something was eating at him, Clay thought. And had been ever since he'd seen Ilene this morning. It had only increased while he'd watched her at the park with her son. Seeing her playing with the boy, laughing, had created an incredible ache in his chest, one he didn't know how to handle.

But he wasn't about to talk about it, at least not until he worked it through in his system. "You mean other than those spicy meatballs?"

Clay nodded toward the large tray of browned meatballs that were still waiting to be plucked up from their perch. The bartender's wife, Greta, had made them. They smelled a great deal better than they tasted, at least to those who were accustomed to better fare.

"The woman tried her best," Andrew said, then grinned. "Can't hold a candle to mine, can they?"

"Nope." Clay watched his father do further justice to the beer he was holding. "And might I add that your modesty is blinding."

"No reason for modesty." Finished, Andrew set down the mug on a nearby table already littered with empty mugs. "Just the facts."

About to comment, Clay held his finger up, stopping his father from continuing. His cell phone was vibrating in his back pocket.

"Hold it, Dad, I'm getting a call, Dad."

Andrew sighed, waving him away to take the call. "No getting away from technology these days, is there?"

"Price you pay for progress." Clay made his way out of the bar to take the call.

"See you at breakfast," Andrew called after him

before turning back to the party and the very inebriated guest of honor.

While Callie and Shaw dropped by the house for breakfast with a fair amount of regularity, Clay, like his twin sister Teri and Rayne, had only to come down the stairs. He'd moved out of the family house with fanfare at twenty-one and grudgingly moved back in approximately six months ago. Circumstances had necessitated it.

The apartment he'd been subletting had been reclaimed by its owner who'd decided to come back to Aurora in order to pursue his career. That left Clay pursuing apartments, not an easy task for a police detective on call most of his days and nights. Especially when his funds were of the limited variety.

Clay was always being generous with his money, an easy touch for friends, or even acquaintances, who found themselves down on their luck. That left him with little money to spend on the things that were important to his own life. Like shelter.

But every weekend found him sitting down with the newspaper, determined to find an apartment that suited his purposes and his pocket, and every Monday found him still home, much to his father's secret contentment.

Though he wouldn't admit it, they all knew that Andrew missed the sound of another male voice in the house. And another male set of hands he could commandeer whenever the whim moved him to undertake yet another remodeling of the house or another much-needed repair project. Unwilling to accept any money from his son in exchange for food and shelter, Andrew took it out in trade. Clay called it slave labor. Both men seemed to be happy with the arrangement, knowing it was only temporary and would change all too soon.

Stepping outside the bar, Clay turned his collar up as the air swirled around him. In contrast to the almost hot atmosphere inside, it was downright cold out here. Standing under the streetlamp, he flipped open his phone. "Cavanaugh."

"Clay?"

Even though the person on the other end had only uttered his name, he knew who it was. Her voice was never far from the recesses of his mind.

And right now he could hear fear echoing in it. "Ilene?"

He heard her sharp intake of breath. "Clay, I think someone's trying to break in."

The address she'd given him was less than fifteen minutes away by car.

He made it in seven.

The Ilene he remembered didn't frighten easily. Which meant that this was serious and not just the figment of an overactive imagination.

He should have stuck with his instincts and kept up watch, he upbraided himself. If she hadn't been so damn adamant about making him leave…

It wasn't an excuse and he knew it.

As he drove, peeling through yellow lights and ones that had just turned red, Clay kept his siren on. With any luck, it would scare away whoever it was who was attempting to break into her house. He tried not to let his imagination run away with him.

It was the longest seven minutes he could ever remember spending.

Pulling up in front of Ilene's fashionable, tidy two story tract house, Clay all but ripped the key out of the ignition. He was out of the car almost before it stopped moving.

Someone raced from the side of the house.

Clay lost no time giving chase.

With a decent lead, the darkly clad figure dashed straight for the entrance in the gray cinder-block wall that led onto the greenbelt beside the development.

He was only a few seconds behind the man, but by the time Clay reached the entrance, he couldn't see anyone in either direction. Whoever had tried to get into Ilene's house had melted into the shadows.

Clay bit off a scalding curse and hurried back to Ilene's house. The lights were on in the front, but he couldn't see any movement through the curtains. He rang the bell. There was no answer.

His heart froze in his chest. Had he caught the perpetrator breaking in or leaving the scene of a crime? Abandoning the bell, he knocked on the door. Pounded on it would have been a more apt description. He wasn't a patient man when agitated.

"Ilene, damn it, it's Clay, open the door."

Taking out microtools that were not exactly smiled upon by the department, he was about to break into Ilene's house himself when he heard the lock on the other side being flipped.

The next moment the door opened. Ilene stood there, her eyes wide with a fear she desperately tried to contain. A fear she was clearly unaccustomed to and hated.

She scanned the area right behind him. The streetlight showed the street to be empty. Ilene held on to the door for support, her knees feeling horribly rubbery. "You came."

Clay walked in, taking command of the situation the way he always did. His voice remained deceptively laid-back. "Protect and serve, that's our motto."

He could see that she was trying to hold herself together as she ran the tip of her tongue over her lips. Only when her breathing was steady did she ask, "Did you see him?"

He nodded. "I saw someone running from the side of the house into the greenbelt. But then I lost him."

Ilene knew how he hated that, hated losing at anything, whether it was a card game or a sporting event. Clay was destined to be a winner and expected to be, no matter what the situation. He'd always equated losing with having a personality flaw. Being part of a large family had made him competitive at a very young age.

Just having him here made her feel better. Stronger. And maybe a little silly for overreacting. But that was partially his fault. He and his cousin had made her believe her life was in danger.

Embarrassed, annoyed at having to ask for help, she shrugged, moving toward the mantel and straightening photographs that were perfectly orderly.

"I'm sorry. I didn't mean to take you away from anything." When he looked at her curiously, she explained, "I heard noise in the background when I called."

Ilene felt herself fumbling for words as if they were covered with slippery soap and she was trying to grasp them with her hands. Damn it, what was happening to her? To her life? She'd always wanted to be in control and now it felt as if everything was spinning all around her.

He hadn't realized that the noise in the bar had followed him out. "No, you didn't take me away from anything. Just a retirement party I was leaving, anyway." He could swear that she looked as if she was about to pass out. The color had suddenly drained from her face. She looked vulnerable, he thought. "Hey, are you all right?"

"Yes, I'm fine," she said defiantly just before she felt herself crumbling inside. She shut her eyes to keep the tears from suddenly leaking out. Where had *they* come from? she thought accusingly. This wasn't like her. She was strong, resourceful.

But he and his cousin had made her think that her baby was in danger, and that changed everything.

"No, I'm not," she admitted. "Someone tried to get in here, Clay. Someone I didn't know or want in my house was trying to break in. They could have scared my son. I—" Her voice cracked and she covered her mouth with her fingertips to keep the sob from breaking free.

"Shhh."

Faced with the promise of tears, not knowing what else to do, Clay did what came naturally. He took Ilene into his arms and held her against him. She struggled for a second before giving in and letting him hold her.

A flood of feelings instantly rushed over him. Six years ago, he was holding her to him because they were wildly, unreasonably in love. Back then, at times like this, he'd find himself loving the moment he was in because she was in it, as well.

And being terrified of that same moment. Because Ilene represented everything that could make him weak, that could make him codependent. Everything that could take his manhood and cut him off at the knees.

She'd had that kind of power over him. Until he'd taken it away from her. But for now she needed comfort, and he needed to be able to give it to her, such as it was.

Stroking her hair, he whispered against it. "It's going to be okay."

Just for a moment Ilene allowed herself to cling to him, to cling to the moment and pretend that he could protect her. Pretend that nothing had changed and she could put her faith and trust in this man who would always be there for her.

But he hadn't been.

And he couldn't be. No one could. He'd proved that to her.

A cold resolve came over her. She couldn't depend on anyone but herself. She was all that Alex had. Which meant she had to be brave for both of them. Being brave meant not falling to pieces.

With effort, she pulled herself together and drew away.

"No, it's not. Nothing's going to be all right, not yet. And nothing is ever going to be the same again." She wiped the heel of her hand against the tears. Tossing her head, she tried to regain some of fragmented composure. For a second she tried to deny the obvious. "Maybe it was just a common burglar."

"Maybe," he said, his eyes on her face. "But you don't believe that."

Another shaky breath left her. She'd never been much for lying, even to herself. "No, I don't believe that."

With a sigh she sank down on the sofa, then rose again, as if there were springs in her legs that wouldn't allow her to relax. She couldn't sit, couldn't remain still. Someone had tried to break in, to harm her. To harm her son. And she was powerless to do anything about it except dial a phone.

Frustration chewed at her. Had Walken actually authorized this? Had the man who'd played Santa Claus at last year's Christmas party, who'd had her son climb up on his knee, given the go-ahead to someone to attempt to break into her house? And do what? Threaten her? Or worse?

Unable to stay still, she began to pace the room again. But there was nowhere to go.

Clay watched her as she prowled about the space. "You want to tell me what happened?"

Talking. Talking about it was good, she thought. Talking about it brought it into the light and maybe would make it fade away. She ran her hands along her arms as she spoke. She was cold.

"I just came down from putting Alex to bed. He likes me to read to him until he falls asleep, and sometimes it takes a while," she said, a hint of a smile playing along her lips as if she was seeking comfort from the familiar act. He could remember when that smile had been his exclusive property. Now it belonged to anyone but him. "I came downstairs to put away the dishes and thought I heard something at the back of the house. There's a sliding glass door that leads out to the back patio," she explained. "When I got there, I didn't see anyone, but then I thought I heard someone walking along the side of the house."

She knew she should have checked it out herself first, but all she could think of was that it would leave Alex alone in the house.

"I thought I heard him rattling the window. I guess I panicked and called you." Her shrug was dismissive as she ran her hands along her arms again. "Maybe it was the wind," she muttered.

"The wind was dressed in black and wore sneakers."

Her last shred of hope tore away from her fingertips. Even so, she fell back on another attempt at denial. She didn't want to believe the worst, not about someone she'd worked so closely with. "Then it was a burglar."

"Or someone trying to blend into the night until he got in. Let me take a look outside, see what I can find. You stay here," he told her sternly as she began to follow him. To his surprise, Ilene nodded her head and remained where she was.

He was back within a few minutes, holding something in his hand. A drawing of some sort. "I don't think whoever it was was trying to break in. He was trying to warn you off."

"Warn me off?" she repeated, puzzled.

In response, Clay held up what he'd found taped to the window she'd heard being rattled. It was a drawing of three monkeys sitting side by side. One covered his mouth, another his ears, the third his eyes. The message was clear.

"This is only the first step. It'll escalate. The next time he'll be inside the house."

She looked at Clay accusingly. "You're scaring me."

"Good," he retorted flatly. "I want to. I also want you to take Janelle's suggestion seriously."

She didn't want to. Janelle's suggestion meant going into hiding. She wanted to stand her ground, to stay in her own home. To continue with her life as if nothing had happened.

But she knew that something *had* happened, and just as she'd said to him when he first came in, nothing was ever going to be the same again.

She couldn't hide her head in the sand. Not when she had Alex to think of. "So what do I do?"

"Well, you can't stay here. We can place you in a hotel and—" Clay began to outline the familiar course of action in these cases. She was a witness and had to be kept alive.

But Ilene was already adamantly shaking her head. "No."

He could feel his temper suddenly getting frayed. No one had that kind of effect on him—except for her. But then, she could always make him feel things no one else could.

"Ilene, this isn't the time to be stubborn."

"I'm not being stubborn. But I won't disrupt Alex's life."

He stared at her. "And having people break into his house and possibly abduct his mother or worse isn't going to disrupt it? Think, Ilene, use your head. This time he was asleep, maybe next time he won't be—"

She wasn't going to let him scare her, at least not any more than she already was. "There's got to be another solution."

Did she think this was some kind of game that if she didn't like it, she could just pick up all the marbles and go home? She'd set something in motion by bringing the audit's discrepancies to light, something that couldn't be stopped. All he could do was get her out of the way of the rolling boulder that threatened to crush her.

"There is."

"What?" she demanded.

He didn't like her tone, didn't like the situation they found themselves in. Didn't like to think what could happen to her if he couldn't convince her. "First you can start by trusting me."

Chapter 4

Ilene looked at the man standing before her for a long moment. How could he ask her to trust him after the history they had?

"If I remember correctly, that was where I made my mistake."

The next moment she forced herself away from the emotional vortex that was sucking her into its midst. The past was over. She had to leave it behind her. She hadn't called him because they had a history, she'd called him because she needed a policeman and he was familiar with what was going on. She hadn't wanted to go into long explanations, she'd just wanted to have someone come quickly.

"Sorry, that was uncalled for." Her voice was crisp, devoid of feeling. Ilene told herself that the only way she was going to get through this was to keep a very tight rein on her emotions. "After all, you're just trying to do your job."

Clay couldn't shake the feeling he was out in the middle of nowhere, trying to find his way through a minefield. "Right, and my job is to keep you and your son safe even if you don't want to be."

Her temper erupted. "I never said I didn't want to be safe. I just don't want to have complete chaos." She thought of her own childhood, of how she'd never felt as if she could count on anything. "A child needs stability in his life, otherwise there's no foundation, nothing to build on."

She could see by the expression on his face that Clay thought she was blowing this all out of proportion.

"And going to a hotel would cause chaos?" He wasn't mocking her, but he might as well have been.

Ilene didn't expect him to understand. He didn't have children. And from what she gathered, his own life had been cushioned by a family that cared about him.

"He has a routine," she insisted. "Kindergarten, friends. If I give up our liberty to a tag-team of policemen, how is that going to make Alex feel? I would be taking him away from everything that's familiar to him."

"Except for the most important ingredient. You," Clay pointed out quietly. "And maybe your son's more resilient than you think." She just continued to look at him, not saying a word. She didn't have to. Her eyes did it for her. Clay sighed, dragging his hand through his hair. He went back to the thought he'd had when she made her initial protest. "Okay, maybe I have an idea."

Here came the trust part, she thought, her eyes never leaving his face. "Like what?"

Even though he was pretty sure his father would go along with this, he knew he couldn't just take it for granted. "Give me a second."

Turning from her, Clay took out his cell phone and pressed a preprogrammed number. It belonged to his father's new cell phone. The cell phone had been an impromptu gift that hadn't been all that warmly received. Andrew maintained that he didn't need a cell phone. That the old-fashioned method of using a stationary telephone was just fine with him.

But Callie and Teri had insisted that he needed to get "with the times" and that this allowed them to always reach him if necessary. The deciding argument that he could also reach them whenever he wanted had finally turned the tide.

Now if his father had only remembered to leave it on, Clay thought, they'd be home free.

The cell phone on the other end rang a total of ten times before the annoying automatic message finally came on. Not bothering to listen to the theory that "the party you are trying to reach is either not answering or currently out of the calling area" Clay closed the phone and then opened it again. He hit redial immediately.

This time he got a response.

"Hello?"

"Dad, it's Clay." There was some kind of din accompanying his father's voice. He wasn't sure, but it sounded like singing. Very bad singing. "Why aren't you answering your phone?"

"Was that you? I thought I heard something ringing, but it's so damn noisy in here, I thought maybe it was just me."

"You're still at the party?" Clay had difficulty picturing his father in that kind of social situation. Ever since his mother had disappeared, his father had become the very core of the family unit. Because he'd become such a fixture, there were times Clay had to remind himself that his father needed to get out among his own kind.

He heard his father chuckle. In the background the noise level picked up. "You're missing a hell of a time. By the way, Adrienne Ballard is asking after you."

Patrol Officer Adrienne Ballard was just one of the scores of women he'd gone out with since his breakup with Ilene. Blond, vibrant and nicely endowed, Adrienne was a woman who knew how to enjoy herself and how not to complicate things by trying to bring up the matter of strings. In short, his kind of woman.

Still, the notion of seeing Adrienne right now did

nothing for him. He tried to tell himself it was because he was on duty but the truth of it was after a handful of dates with the woman, he'd found himself getting bored, wanting to move on. She hadn't kept his mind occupied—the way Ilene had.

"That's nice," he said dismissively. "Listen, Dad, I need a favor."

"Ask."

That he was one of the lucky ones was once again brought home to him. His father was always there, always willing to help. Clay knew by experience that not too many people could say that about either of their parents.

"How do you feel about having a houseguest? Two," he amended, remembering the boy sleeping upstairs.

"Two?" The long pause on the other end surprised Clay. "Look, Clay, this is just as much your house as it is mine, you know that, but, call me old-fashioned, I draw the line at something kinky—"

The seriousness of the situation eroded for a moment as Clay struggled not to laugh. Obviously, his father thought of him as a wild stud. "Dad, Dad, hold it. It's not like that. I need a safe place for a friend and her little boy."

There was relief in the sigh Clay heard. "Oh, sure. When?"

"Now." Clay kept his fingers mentally crossed.

His father didn't disappoint him. "Right. I can be home in about fifteen minutes."

Clay grinned. The man was a rock. He should have known there was nothing to worry about.

"Thanks, Dad." Time to launch into the second phase of his plan. "Do you know if Shaw and Callie are still at the party?"

"Callie left with Brent, but Shaw's still here." Andrew made no effort to disguise his curiosity. "Why?"

Clay glanced toward Ilene and wasn't surprised to see that she appeared to be listening to every word. Why shouldn't she? It was her future that was being bandied about here. "I'm going to need decoys."

This time the pause was pregnant, as if Andrew was entertaining various scenarios. "Is it that serious?"

"I wouldn't be doing this if it wasn't."

"Well, I don't know where Rayne is, I never do with that girl, but I did see Teri a few minutes ago, will she do?"

All three of his sisters had basically the same height and coloring. Their hair was lighter than Ilene's, but their builds were similar and they just needed the suggestion of Ilene, not an exact duplicate. "Just as good. I'll give them each a call. See you in a little while."

Clay rang off. But before he could start punching in his brother's cell phone number, Ilene placed her hand on his wrist. "Why do you need decoys?"

He saw the heightened state of alert in her eyes.

Despite her protest, maybe she was finally beginning to see how really serious the situation was.

"Because if I'm right, they might still be watching the house, waiting for me to leave. If I leave with you, they're going to follow." He saw her brow furrow. "But not if they think we've already left."

"I don't understand."

He didn't have time to go over the particulars. There were things left to do. "Just leave it all to me." He·flashed her a smile. "Think of it as your tax dollars at work."

She dropped her hand from his wrist. Like an arrow with a homing device, the smile he'd flashed at her had gone right through her. She doubted that he knew the effect he still had on her, and there was no way in hell she was ever going to let him even guess. But having him in charge of the situation did make her feel better.

"Why don't you go and throw a few things together for you and the boy? Take some of his favorite toys so he doesn't feel so uprooted," he added.

"I'm whisking him out of his bed in the middle of the night. How can't he feel uprooted?" she challenged. She stared at the drawing he'd taken down from her window. Clay was right, even if this was just a warning, it had spooked her. And it could only escalate from here.

"Because you're whisking him away to another

home. Trust me, he won't be traumatized. My father's very good with kids.''

"Your father?''

''I thought you and the boy could stay with him. Dad's good with kids,'' he repeated before he turned away to call his brother.

Within a few minutes he had everything arranged.

''Is this really necessary?''

Ilene left the question open to anyone who wanted to answer it. Clay had just admitted two people into her house via the patio door. From what she could ascertain, the man and woman had entered via the backyard. Which meant that they had to climb over the fence, coming from one of her neighbor's yards. How could they have done that without being detected?

The same way whoever had left that warning had, she told herself. He'd been in her backyard before she'd heard him.

Nothing seemed safe anymore.

''This is all so cloak-and-dagger,'' she protested when no one answered her question.

The woman was the first to speak. Her eyes were kind and her smile looked as if it had been lifted directly from Clay's face.

''A lot more cloak, a lot less dagger,'' she laughed. Extending her hand, she took Ilene's in hers. ''Hi, I'm Teri. Clay and I are twins,'' she said in response to the quizzical look creasing Ilene's brow. Then winked. "But I'm the pretty one."

The man standing next to her looked as if he could be another twin, as well, except that he appeared to be a little older. "Shaw Cavanaugh." He nodded his head toward his siblings. "They're both homely enough to stop clocks," he interjected. "We all know the family looks ran out after me."

This wasn't the time for an exchange of vague pleasantries, even though Clay did want to see the tension leave Ilene's shoulders. Right now, she looked like a woman doing a tightrope crossing over an open cage of hungry lions.

"We'll do introductions and snappy patter later," Clay told them crisply. "You bring the doll?"

Teri nodded, producing it out of the backpack she'd brought with her. "Took a little digging."

Clay's eyebrows drew together as he looked at the doll in question. "That looks like Miss Betsy." Miss Betsy had been his youngest sister, Rayne's, cherished first doll. She and the doll had been inseparable, and she'd carried it around until the clothes that had come with the doll had all but disintegrated. Callie had sewn her a new outfit.

"First one I could find in the garage," Teri answered glibly. "You said you were in a hurry and that it needed to be about the size of a four-year-old," she reminded him. There was only one way the doll could remotely pass the test. Teri turned to Ilene. "Do you have a blanket handy?"

Ilene looked around before she spotted the light crocheted afghan she kept on the sofa. Alex liked to cuddle up beneath it early on Saturday mornings to watch cartoons. Fetching it, she brought it back. "Is this what you have in mind?"

Teri quickly wrapped the throw around the doll.

"Perfect," Teri pronounced, laying the doll on the table. She scrutinized Ilene quickly, then glanced down to see that the other woman was wearing high heels. "We're probably about the same height," Teri judged. "I'm going to need to borrow one of your coats. Preferably with a hood if you have one."

Ilene went to the hall closet where she kept her outerwear. She took out a parka that she favored, as well as a jacket for Alex. All the while, Ilene felt as if she was moving through water, as if she was sleepwalking, trapped in someone else's dream.

Or someone else's nightmare.

Ilene held out the parka to the other woman. "This do?"

Teri nodded. "It'll do fine." Shedding her own jacket, Teri quickly put on the one Ilene had brought to her as Clay and Shaw conferred on the side. The buzz of lowered voices was obviously getting their star performer edgy, she thought. "It's going to be all right," she promised Ilene.

And then Teri looked past the woman and toward the living room. There, his head drooping over to one side as he sat where he'd been placed on the sofa, was a little dark-haired boy, sound asleep amid all the activity.

Teri's expression softened to the consistency of margarine left out on the kitchen counter way after breakfast was over. "That him?"

Ilene nodded. "Alex."

"Nice name." Teri quickly buttoned up the jacket and looked back to the woman whose life was getting tossed upside down. They had no details, not even a name for the woman. Only that Clay needed a favor. That was enough for any of them. "Don't worry, it'll all be over with soon."

Ilene tried to smile. The shaky sigh escaped before she could stop it. "Not soon enough for me."

"Are you about set?" Clay directed the question to his sister as he handed Shaw the keys to the car he'd left parked out front.

Shaw gave him his own. "My car's parked in front of the house diagonally behind this one. It's the one with the California pepper tree out in front." He looked at his sister. Teri slipped the parka over her head and picked up the bundled doll, then nodded. "Give us about ten minutes," Shaw told Clay.

A sliver of impatience clawed at Clay. "I know how to do this. I'm the one who called you."

Shaw looked from his brother to Ilene. He then gave Clay's hair a playful tousle, the way he had when they were younger and he was establishing order. Except now they were equals. "Just imparting a little wisdom, little brother,'' Shaw told him with a grin.

''Well, that'll fill a thimble or two,'' Teri cracked. ''C'mon, let's go. I want to get back to the party. My beer's getting warm.''

''Ah, the flower of youth,'' Shaw commented with a shake of his head.

Lowering her head, Teri tightened her arms around the bundle, holding it against her with all the care a mother would give to her sleeping child. Shaw was right beside her, his arm wrapped around her protectively as he guided mother and child out.

Just before he closed the door, he shut off the last of the lights.

The darkness bathed them. Straining her eyes against it, Ilene looked toward the sofa where her son was still dozing. She didn't want him suddenly waking up and panicking. Alex was afraid of the dark.

For a moment there was nothing, only darkness and the sound of Ilene breathing. Clay tried not to remember the last time that sound had wafted to him in the stillness of the night. Tried not to remember making love with Ilene until the sun began to slowly slip its fingers into the room, poking into the corners, coaxing away the shadows.

He tried but he failed. The memories came, anyway.

Maybe, he thought, when you made love with the right woman, it was a little like riding a bicycle. No matter how much time actually went by, when you come into the proximity of a bicycle, you can't help but recall the feeling.

The same went for the woman.

Along with her breathing, he could feel her tension fill the air. Inbred instincts made him want to comfort her. ''You all right?''

She ran her tongue along dry lips. It didn't help. ''I've been better,'' she confessed. ''I'm just worried about Alex.''

Kids could handle anything, as long as they had love, he thought. He'd learned that firsthand. ''Don't be. He's going to think of this as one big adventure,'' Clay promised.

''Right.''

She stiffened as she felt Clay's arm slip around her shoulder. He was still wearing that same cologne, the one she'd given him so long ago. The scent stirred memories she wanted to forget. She couldn't handle them and this, too.

She was as stiff as a lightning rod. ''Just me,'' Clay told her softly, ''offering moral support.''

She didn't want him offering moral support. She didn't want him offering anything at all. She didn't want him back in her life, no matter how professionally. Because she couldn't think of him that way.

Ilene clenched her hands at her sides. ''I should have never done this,'' she said regretfully. If there was a way to click her heels and undo everything, she would have. "All I was supposed to do was just sign off on the report, not start going into the figures myself."

He knew her, knew she didn't sweep things under the rug or do things by half measures. If something bore her name, she had to make sure it was right. She had integrity and that meant something to her. He wanted her to be proud of herself, not angry. "Why did you start going into the figures yourself?"

"Because they didn't look right." She sighed. When was she going to learn she couldn't be a crusader? Not anymore. She had a son, a life that had been entrusted to her, she couldn't just think of herself anymore. "Because I didn't want anyone buying stock under false pretenses."

She heard him laugh softly and the sound wound its way to her belly, upsetting it even further. "You always did worry about everyone else."

"And look where it got me."

He didn't like the fatalistic tone in her voice. That wasn't like her. He remembered her as being feisty. She needed to draw on that now. "It's not over."

She covered her face for a second as a myriad of regrets assaulted her. She struggled for high ground. "That's what I'm afraid of."

"What happened to all that optimism you used to have?"

She turned to him and could just about make out his eyes. "It got dried up along the way."

And he had been the one who'd dried it, he thought suddenly. Or was at least responsible for some of it drying up.

He was reading too much into it, Clay told himself. The man who had fathered her child had to be at least partially responsible for her attitude, as well.

Where was he?

Who was he? Had she loved him? Did she still love him?

Clay shut down his mind. There was no sense in going that route, in torturing himself with questions that might never be answered, questions he had no right to ask in the first place. He'd given her up. Willingly. That meant he had no claim to her now, and certainly not the time they'd been apart.

"That's too bad," he finally responded. Glancing down at his watch, he angled it so that the thin beam of moonlight struggling into the room highlighted the golden face. "We'd better get going. You ready?"

She nodded, her mouth suddenly twice as dry as it had been a moment ago. Going over to the sofa, she scooped Alex up in her arms.

Rousing, the small weight shifted against her, like a little monkey seeking a bit of comfort. "Mama?" he mumbled against her chest.

She stroked his head. She wouldn't be able to stand it if she'd put even one hair of his head in danger, she thought.

"It's okay honey, we're going on a little trip." It

had been what she'd told him when he'd looked up at her with sleepy eyes as she'd hurriedly dressed him less than half an hour ago.

"De-neyland?"

"Not yet—" she laughed softly, pressing her to him, drawing comfort from the warmth of his little body against hers "—but soon."

Clay was beside her. "Disneyland a big deal with him?"

She turned her head, whispering even though she knew the boy was asleep again. Bless him, he could sleep through an earthquake once he was in the right mode. "He's never been," she explained. "But he's seen the commercials and he's determined to go."

Something stirred within him, something apart from his sense of duty and the odd nostalgia that pushed its way forward. Something that had to do with children and families and a life on its way to being misspent.

"Maybe when this is all behind you, I'll take the two of you to Disneyland."

No, she wasn't going to allow Clay to seduce her with words, with images that flashed temptingly through her mind. She didn't need or want anything from him beyond protection for her son. "That's okay," she replied crisply. "When this is all behind me, I'll take my son to Disneyland myself."

Clay shrugged. "Whatever you say."

He didn't like her defensive tone, the one that was holding up and waving the No Trespassing sign in front of him, even though he knew that he had at least partly earned it.

"Yes," she replied tersely, "whatever I say."

He first picked up the laptop she insisted on taking with her and then the suitcase she had hurriedly packed for the two of them. Inside was the note he'd taken down from her dining room window. With any luck, there might be a print on it. At least he could hope.

Taking her arm, he directed her to the rear of the house. "Let's get going."

He didn't have to tell her again.

Chapter 5

If the tension were any thicker within Shaw's four-door, unmarked vehicle, it would have been a solid entity. Clay searched for a way to distract the woman on his right who sat staring straight ahead, as rigid as the principles of right and wrong that had brought her to this juncture.

He glanced again in the rearview mirror. His line of vision shifted from the vacant area beyond the rear of the car to the small figure in the back seat. Alex was secured in place with a seat belt, but the boy was still of an age where car seats were the norm. He'd seen the look of concern on Ilene's face when she'd strapped her son in.

"My father has an old car seat in the garage." Clay remembered stumbling across it not that long ago, wondering if his father was saving it for his first grandchild. "I think it was Rayne's."

For a second, she didn't realize that Clay was talking to her. Lost in her own thoughts, in fears that she was struggling to make sense of, it took Ilene a moment to replay the words that had been directed toward her. "What?"

Watching the car in the rearview mirror as he made a left-hand turn, Clay waited until it continued straight before answering. The car hadn't been following him. Better paranoid than sorry later.

"A car seat. For your son." Glancing at her, he saw no indication that she was following him. "We didn't exactly have time to switch the one from your car to Shaw's," he reminded her.

Ilene's complexion looked almost translucent, he thought, even factoring in the limited light from the passing streetlamps. She looked pale and drawn and worried. Not that he could blame her. He knew what it was like, having a world you thought secure suddenly upended. For him it had been his mother's death. It was all you could do to keep from going under.

Ilene shook her head. What was he doing, talking about car seats and the weather? "Rain?"

"Rayne. Lor-rayne," he enunciated slowly. "My youngest sister. We call her Rayne because when Teri was a little girl, she couldn't say Lorrayne. She wasn't as advanced as I was." His joke fell flat, not even coaxing a smile from Ilene. He hated seeing her like this. She didn't deserve to be frightened, to feel like a fugitive for doing the right thing. "If you ask me," he continued in an easy voice, "Dad should have found a way to keep her strapped into it until she was about nineteen. She gave him a lot of grief."

Ilene tried to keep her mind on the conversation and not on the huge knot that had formed in her stomach. "But not anymore?"

Clay felt himself smiling. There was a bet he would have lost. He had figured that nothing would ever get the youngest Cavanaugh to fly right, much less actually join the police department. Showed what he knew.

"She straightened out." The amber light turned red before he could get into the intersection. He raised his eyes to the rearview again. Nothing. Good. "We all did. Fine, upstanding citizens, the lot of us."

Beside him, he heard Ilene laugh softly under her breath. He'd forgotten how much he liked that sound, how it bathed over him, making him want more. "What's so funny?"

She shook her head. Wisps of strawberry-blond hair brushed against either cheek. She combed them away with her fingers. "I don't see you as that."

"Oh?" The light turned green and he took his foot from the brake. "And what do you see me as?"

Not with me, for one thing. "Free." She thought a minute, then added, "Unencumbered."

He saw no contradiction. "Free spirits can be upstanding." His mouth curved. The term was one that always came to mind when he thought of his youngest sister. "Matter of fact, that probably best describes Rayne. I don't think she's ever going to settle down." She was too independent, too bullheaded for that matter. "Much to my father's dismay. I've got this feeling he sees himself at the head of this overpopulated dynasty, having all of us turn up at the table with our assorted spouses and a gaggle of kids."

"Gaggle?" She looked at him. "Isn't that what you call a gathering of geese?"

Clay shrugged as he took another turn. This was the long way home, but he wanted to be certain that there was no one following him. "Gaggle, bunch, herd, you get the idea."

"Yes, I do." Ilene set her mouth grimly. "That you think children are animals."

Conversations from the past returned to her. Clay had made a point of saying he never wanted to settle down, never wanted children. That kids didn't belong in a world that wasn't stable. She'd agreed with him, but that didn't change the fact that in her heart, she'd always wanted at least one child of her own if not more.

"They can be," he said. And then he thought of his father. At what he'd endured at Rayne's hands. The air between the two had been as volatile as a tray filled with nitroglycerin. "They can also be a huge emotional drain on you. Look at what my father went through.''

She had absolutely no idea what his father had gone through. When they'd been together, Clay had never shared that part of himself. What he'd shared was the moment. ''Ever ask him if he regretted it?''

Clay watched the road ahead intently. For the umpteenth time he wondered where his father had found the strength to go on. If he'd loved a woman the way his father had loved his mother and then lost her, he didn't think he would have been able to go on. ''Maybe not now, but he must have somewhere along the line.''

It was Ilene's turn to shrug. ''Everybody regrets even the best of things somewhere along the line.'' She remembered how she'd felt when she discovered she was pregnant. In theory, she'd always hoped the day would come. In reality, it had come at the least opportune time, a frightening prospect when she was least prepared for it. But she'd managed and had lived to be grateful. ''A celebrity busts her tail to get to the point where she's rich and famous, then yearns for when she was unknown and could go to the grocery store unnoticed. To find out if you're really happy with how things have turned out, you have to look at the big picture.''

He surprised her by turning toward her as they came to another stop. ''So, what about your big picture, Ilene? Are you happy?''

In her case, she didn't look at the big picture,

because that should have included someone to love her who measured taller than three feet. Instead, she looked at the small, precious picture, at her world captured in Alex's eyes.

"I love my son." And then, just as it had the past two days, events came up to haunt her. "And up until last week, I loved my job. I was good at it, good at details, at order." She turned her face away from him. A note akin to cynicism came into her voice. She'd been so close to finally getting to the top, and now she was back to square one. Maybe even below square one. "I guess I can't exactly expect a letter of recommendation from Simplicity now."

"Sometimes a clear conscience is better than a letter of recommendation," Clay said.

"Since when did you get philosophical?"

Without a philosophical approach, what he had seen during the course of his police work would have made him quit almost before he ever signed on.

"The job does that to you. We all develop some kind of defense mechanisms. We have to, and philosophy is a hell of a lot better than drinking yourself under the table every night just to be able to keep the nightmares at bay."

Was he just talking, or had his work changed him? By how much? For the better?

Not your business anymore, Ilene.

"I always thought staying one step ahead of a

commitment was your defense mechanism.'' Ilene blew out a breath. He was trying to help her, help her son, and she was being bitchy. "Sorry, I shouldn't have said that. My mind is in a hundred places right now."

"You're entitled," he told her.

He never stewed over anything for very long, firmly believing that was the shortest route to an ulcer. Making the next right, he glanced in the mirror. So far, so good. He wondered if he was getting too complacent. Had he missed anything?

She turned around in her seat to look behind her. The street stretched out, long and dark. "You keep looking in the rearview mirror. You think anyone's following us?"

"Doesn't look that way." He was glad to be able to level with her. "Shaw and Teri should be checking into a motel right about now." The car he'd seen parked in the vicinity had followed after them. With luck, that was the only tail. "They're going to stay there and keep up the ruse for a few hours to hopefully buy you a little time." He grinned, sparing her a glance before looking back on the road. "Whoever tried to scare you off isn't going to expect you to come home with the police,"

She laughed again. "I didn't expect to be coming home with the police, either." She folded her hands in front of her. It annoyed her that they still shook a little. "I appreciate you doing this, I know this isn't business as usual for you."

"It never was with you." The words had just slipped out. When she looked at him sharply, he got into his cop mode. "You realize you can't get in contact with anyone while you're at my father's house."

"I realize that." Did he think she was stupid? That she'd get on the phone and call a girlfriend? Damn, she had to stop being so defensive. He was just doing his best. More. "There's no one to call."

Clay looked back at the boy. "Not even Alex's father?"

Ilene pulled back. The ice beneath her feet cracked a little. She couldn't relax her guard for a moment. "Alex's father isn't in the picture."

"Whose idea was that?"

She stuck to the truth as much as she could, wishing he'd drop the subject. "Mine."

He'd felt more than seen her stiffen. His training had him reading her body language. "Was he abusive?"

Ilene gave him one of the reasons she'd given herself for keeping him out of Alex's life. "No, but having him coming in and out of Alex's life whenever the whim moved him would have been detrimental to Alex."

"And he's okay with this?"

"He has to be." Feeling progressively more uncomfortable, she shifted in her seat. "Look, do we have to talk about this?"

"No, we can talk about anything you want." He

was just trying to get her to forget for a little while why she was here in the first place. "How long have you been back in town?"

"How did you know I left town?" As soon as she'd discovered she was pregnant, she'd known she couldn't stay and run the risk of running into Clay. Seeing her, he would have guessed he was Alex's father. So she'd gone to stay with a friend until she'd gotten on her feet and struck out on her own.

"Because I tried to look you up about a month after our breakup."

She hadn't expected that. "Guilt?"

Probably in part. Since he was responsible for her finally giving him his walking papers. He'd orchestrated it, and once the melody ceased to play, he'd found himself battling regret and guilt at the same time. "I just wanted to see how you were doing."

"I was doing fine," she told him, saying lines she'd rehearsed over and over again years ago. "Took a job with Simplicity at one of their branch offices in Denver. Did so fine that they transferred me to their regional headquarters."

She didn't add how much soul searching she had done before accepting the promotion, battling the very real concern she had at the possibility of running into him if she accepted the job. She'd almost turned the promotion down, but the options for a single mother trying to make a career for herself and her son were still not that plentiful that she could afford to walk away from something as lucrative as the offer had promised to be.

Certainly walking away from it now, aren't you?

He studied her profile and tried to fill in blanks. There was something she wasn't telling him. Why should she, he argued. It wasn't as if they'd just drifted apart; he'd ripped them apart. At the bottom of a bottle of very fine Kentucky bourbon, he'd come face-to-face with the reasons why some time back. He was afraid of loving someone. Afraid that they'd be taken away from him the way his mother had been taken away from his father. From him.

He made the logical assumption. "So Alex's father doesn't live in Aurora."

She looked at him. "Why are you suddenly so interested in Alex's father?"

Ilene wasn't even sure why she was asking him that instead of shutting down the subject again. Maybe it was because she wanted him to make her believe that if Alex had been his child, he would have wanted to know about it. Maybe she wanted him to say something to convince her that she'd made a mistake in not telling him and that he truly wanted a child. Wanted her.

Damn it, she was letting all this get to her. She was punchy and tired and unreasonable, Ilene told herself. Why else was she hoping to hear something she knew she hadn't a chance in hell of hearing? Clay was Clay. A footloose, fancy-free bachelor who made no bones about telling a woman right up front where he stood. There'd been no deception, no promises to feel cheated about. He'd been honest to her from the start.

The only thing was, she'd wanted him to change his mind. Because of her. And he hadn't.

He lifted a shoulder, letting it drop carelessly. "Just wondering what kind of man would walk away from you."

An enigmatic smile played on her lips. "Maybe you should angle that rearview mirror down a little lower," she suggested.

He'd asked for that one, Clay thought. "Yeah, well, maybe I've had some thoughts about that, too."

She felt her heart suddenly rise to attention. "Such as?"

Warning signals went up. He was going places he couldn't back out of. But then he saw his reprieve. Clay nodded toward the well-lit house up ahead, at the end of the block. "We're here."

She'd been so intent, waiting for an answer, that she didn't follow him for a second. "Here?"

"My house." He nodded at it again. "My father's house."

But she'd heard just one thing. Something inside of her, a vein intent on self-preservation, came to life. "What do you mean your house?"

He slowed as an orange cat dashed across the street. Lincoln was older than the hills and by all rights should have been dead years ago.

"I guess I forgot to tell you, I'm staying here, too. Temporarily." he said.

Somehow, it didn't seem quite right for a twenty-seven-year-old police detective to be living at home with his father and two sisters. Although he had to admit that, if he didn't care what other people thought, he didn't really mind the living arrangements. The sounds of his family around him gave off comforting vibes. If he wanted to be alone, he could usually manage it, and if he didn't, there was always someone to talk to.

Clay wondered if that made him a family man or just someone who had trouble moving on and away from a good thing.

No, he reminded himself, he'd left Ilene behind, and that was definitely moving away from a good thing.

Ilene hesitated as doubt grew larger. "Maybe this wasn't such a good idea."

"If you have any concerns, my father is pretty much of a fixture in the house. He'll be your buffer. And my sisters are here when they're off duty." He stopped the car and looked at her. He couldn't read the expression on her face, couldn't find his way around her eyes the way he'd been able to do so often when they'd been together. "This isn't a den of iniquity, Ilene, this is a place to keep you and your son very safe."

Even as he said it, she knew it was true. Not necessarily because he said it, but because of the distinguished, gray-haired man who was standing in front of the house, framed by the illumination coming from the front porch light.

The moment they pulled up in the driveway, Andrew Cavanaugh came down the stairs, a ready smile on his remarkably unlined face. She could see the resemblance as he approached the car. This was what Clay would look like in another thirty years.

Opening the passenger door, Andrew took her hand to help her out. "You must be Ilene." His voice was warm, welcoming.

"Yes, I am," she heard herself reply. She felt instantly at ease, as if she was in the presence of someone she could turn to with anything. It amazed her that someone she'd never met could make her feel that, just by the warmth of his smile.

"Welcome to my house," he told her, his attention on the sleeping child in the back. "What is he, about five?"

"Four." She hated lying. But if she said five, then Clay could easily do the math, easily realize that she had conceived Alex while they were still together.

"Big for his age." Before she could say anything, Andrew had already opened the rear door and was scooping the boy out. "Been a long time since I held one of these in my arms." Expertly he took the boy out without waking him. Looking at Ilene, he observed, "His hair's dark."

As dark as Clay's was, she thought. Ilene pressed

her lips together, wondering what the man was thinking. "His father had dark hair."

Andrew's eyes traveled toward his younger son a moment before he turned toward the front step. "Handsome boy," he pronounced before walking back into the house.

Clay came up beside her. He held her suitcase in one hand, the laptop tucked under his arm. With his free hand he took her arm and guided her up the stairs in his father's wake.

Panic reared its head, pushing aside the sense of well-being within her that Andrew had begun to build. "I don't want to impose—"

Andrew heard her. "Impose?" There was an incredulous expression on his face as he turned to look at her. Holding Alex against him, he closed the door with his free hand. "I've got enough rooms in the house to turn it into a hotel," he told her softly. "My two oldest are gone, and there are guest rooms besides that. You're not imposing, girl, you're keeping us from getting lonely." He pointedly looked at his son over Alex's head. "Isn't that right, Clay?"

Clay set the suitcase down for a moment. "Whatever you say, Dad."

"That's a first," Andrew commented, his words directed to the young woman his son had brought to him. "Usually, he likes nothing better than to butt heads with me. You partial to the first or the second floor, Ilene? I've got an empty bedroom on each."

"First," she said. It made her feel as if she could

leave if she wanted to. Instantly she felt guilty at
wanting to flee. The man was putting himself out on
her account, and he didn't even know her.

She followed him as he led the way to the rear
of the house. He was still carrying her son. "You're
being incredibly accommodating."

"Hear that, Clay?" Turning to look at his son
over his shoulder, Andrew grinned. "I'm accommodating." There were times when some, if not all,
of his children thought of him as pigheaded and
stubborn. They'd all tried, at one time or another, to
gently talk him into accepting Rose's death. But he
refused. Because he knew she was alive.

"Sure, Dad." Clay gave his father a look.

Andrew shook his head. "Teach your son early
on never to talk back." He shifted the boy in his
arms, a smile of appreciation as he did so. Even the
simple gesture made it clear that the man ached for
a grandchild. "It's something I overlooked doing.
Not that you can teach this one anything." He
frowned in Clay's direction. "Stubborn as a mule
most of the time."

She couldn't help smiling. "I know."

"Then you do know each other?" Stopping in
front of a doorway, Andrew turned to look at her as
he waited for an answer.

She took a breath before saying quietly, "A very
long time ago."

Okay, time to get the train back on the track. Clay
elbowed his way in between his father and Ilene.

''Dad, I didn't bring Ilene here so you could practice interrogating someone.''

''Just being friendly, Clay. Something that comes naturally to me if not you.'' He walked into one of the two guest rooms. ''Here you go. I think you'll be very comfortable here.'' Very gently he placed Alex down in the middle of the bed. ''The bathroom's right through there,'' he indicated a door inside the bedroom. ''And the kitchen's just down the hall. Speaking of which, is there anything I can get you?''

She shook her head. ''No, you've already been more than kind.''

''Something warm to drink?'' he suggested, then thought of the state her nerves were probably in. ''Or maybe something a little stronger to calm your nerves? Just this once,'' he tacked on, guessing at the protest rising to her lips.

Clay knew it was time to come to her rescue before his father started force-feeding her. ''Her nerves are fine, Dad.''

Crossing back to the doorway, Andrew snorted. ''Can't see how that's possible when she made the trip here with you driving.''

''Dad—''

Andrew raised his hands in front of him in mock, grudging surrender. ''Backing away.'' He cocked his head, looking around his son to his new house guest. ''You've got the run of the place, Ilene. Feel free to use it.''

"Thank you."

"I'd better let you get some rest," Clay mumbled, half hoping she'd ask him to remain. But she didn't, as he knew she wouldn't, and he withdrew.

Ilene closed the door behind him.

"Like her smile," Andrew said as they walked away from the room. Behind them, they heard her flip the lock. "Pretty girl."

"Yes," Clay agreed. And she'd only gotten more so, he thought. He looked at his father. "Thanks for letting them stay here."

Andrew waved away the thanks and began to head for the stairs. "Don't mention it." Hand on the banister, he paused. "By the way."

Clay raised his eyebrow, waiting. "Yes?"

"Is the boy yours?"

Chapter 6

"What?"

Clay felt as if he could have easily been knocked over by a moderate-size feather. Especially since his father had given voice to the question floating in the recesses of his own mind.

Stopping dead in his tracks, Clay looked at his father.

"You know I don't like to pry—"

Clay snorted. "Yeah, right, and you're also a misguided leprechaun."

Amusement played on Andrew's lips. "Whole other discussion, boy. Now—"

"No." Time to nip this thing in the bud before his father got carried away.

Arching the same eyebrow that each of his children were prone to raising, Andrew looked far from convinced. "No?"

"No, he's not my son," Clay said firmly. He didn't want to have to tell his father to butt out, but he would if it came to that. "Alex is four. I wasn't seeing her five years ago. We'd broken up by then."

Andrew leaned against the wall, his arms crossed in front of a chest that still looked powerful. "Kind of big for four."

Clay found himself playing devil's advocate, taking the exact oppose stance from the one he'd mentally taken earlier. "Some kids are."

"Boy has your coloring."

Clay saw the end of his temper in sight and struggled to hold on to the rope. "That narrows it down to about a quarter of the kids in Aurora." And then he laughed. No, he wasn't Alex's father, for all the reasons he cited and more. If he'd gotten Ilene pregnant, she wouldn't have kept something like that from him. She would have told him. She was nothing if not honest. "I get around, Dad, but I'd have to sweep through the town like a broom to leave that much of myself around."

"I'm not asking about the town, I'm asking about a woman who looks at you as if this isn't the first time she's seen you."

When he'd asked his father if Ilene could stay at the house, he hadn't mentioned that he'd known her before, much less that they'd been involved. He hadn't confided in his father back then. Maybe because Clay had known from the start that this time was different.

Now Clay just shook his head. "You should have never retired from the force, Dad. You need something to occupy your mind."

Andrew grinned as he looked past Clay's head toward the room they had just walked out of. "Might say I've found it." And then he glanced at his watch. "Where the hell is your sister?"

His father didn't have to say which sister he was referring to. Teri was at the motel, still playing decoy with Shaw. Even if she hadn't been, Teri was the reliable one, just like Callie was. His father hardly ever worried about either of them. Rayne was another story. "Relax, Dad, Rayne's a big girl now."

Andrew gave him a penetrating look, as if to ask how that was supposed to be a comfort to him. "That's exactly why I can't relax. That new leaf she turned over might want to blow itself back someday."

At least the conversation had gotten away from the subject of Alex's paternity. But once his father got started on Rayne and her escapades, Clay knew he could go on forever. A retreat was called for.

Clay pretended to stretch. "Well, it's been a long day. I'm going to turn in."

Just as he moved to pass his father, Andrew commandeered his arm. Keeping a firm grasp on it, he directed his son toward the kitchen where lengthy conversations were coaxed out with rich, hot food and, according to Callie, the best coffee this side of heaven. "Not before filling me in you're not."

Clay blew out a breath. "Dad, I already told you, he's not mine."

"I know, I know, the timing's off. I mean fill me in on the particulars about this case."

You could take the man out of the police force, but you couldn't take the police force out of the man. Clay shook his head, knowing he was in for an even longer night than he'd anticipated. But that was all right, he decided philosophically, because he had a feeling that sleep would not come easily tonight. Not when Ilene was sleeping somewhere in the same house that he was.

He grinned at his father, allowing himself to be led into the kitchen. "You *really* should never have left the force."

"An obsessive cop tends to make people nervous, especially when he's in a position of higher authority."

Clay slipped onto a stool at the long granite bar that ran on the other side of the work island. He knew his father was referring to his belief that his mother was still alive. At one point, his father had spent all his free time going over the evidence, trying to find someone who might have seen his wife leaving the area around the river, or someone who might have talked to her before she had taken off.

The newspapers had been unfair to Andrew, making it seem as if she had been fleeing her husband when she'd accidentally plowed her car over the bridge into the river. But when they'd recovered the vehicle, there'd been no suitcase, no prior arrangements made, no credit card charges to indicate that she was doing anything more than just going off on a long drive to cool off after a heated argument.

An argument, Clay had discovered recently, that had been over his uncle. Not the one who was currently chief of detectives, but the one who'd died not too long after Rose Cavanaugh had gone missing. Uncle Mike, he'd learned through something his cousin Patrick, Mike's son, had overheard, had been attempting to get Rose to run away with him.

That day she disappeared, had she been going to meet him? Had something happened to prevent her from getting to Mike?

Clay shook his head, shaking off the thoughts. He was beginning to sound like his father. And he already had enough on his mind with his own ghost from the past.

An ironic smile played along his lips as he wondered just how much of an effect the one had on the other. If his mother hadn't walked out, if she'd stayed home, stayed alive, would he still feel this rootless when it came to making a lasting commitment? Would pledging his heart to just one woman for all time be easier for him?

It was something he knew he was never going to resolve. Better not to try.

He looked at his father now. "You weren't obsessive, Dad. Just stubborn. As always."

Andrew took a plate of home-made pastries and placed it on the counter in front of Clay before sliding onto a stool beside him. "You know, sometimes you do have a lot of insight, boy."

She'd remained in bed as long as she could, hoping to drift off again, to grab another snatch of sleep. But after an hour of futile attempts, Ilene gave up and got dressed. The moment she did, Alex had woken up, as fresh and rested as she was not. So she'd gotten them both dressed and then, holding his hand more for her own support than for his, she'd ventured out to the kitchen.

There were pots and pans everywhere, all being used by the whirling dervish in the middle of the room. Wonderful smells greeted her; however, she was more curious about the explosion of toys in the family room just beyond the kitchen. The place was absolutely littered with them. It didn't seem to be a natural state of affairs for a house full of adults only.

But then it occurred to her that Andrew Cavanaugh might be a grandfather several times over. She didn't know that much about the man. Or that much about Clay's family, when she came down to it. Not much beyond the fact there were a lot of people in it. Unlike hers. She had no aunts, no uncles and consequently, no cousins.

And hardly even parents, she thought ruefully.

They'd each gone on to remarry and form new bonds, all which excluded her.

Alex pulled at her side, eager to get at the treasure trove spread out before him. She tightened her fingers around his. Though she'd been officially up for the past half hour, she still felt a little groggy. But that was because she'd gotten less than four hours total sleep last night. Unlike her son, she didn't adjust all that well to different sleeping conditions. And it didn't exactly help that her mind kept insisting on racing along a mile a minute, trying to process everything that had gone on yesterday. Not the least of which was having Clay reenter her life.

He wasn't reentering, she insisted silently, he was there in a professional capacity only. It wasn't his fault that she'd felt that old electricity shooting through her at top speed the moment he'd lightly placed his hand on her arm. That was strictly her problem and she was going to have to do something about it before she joined the ranks of the living dead.

She had more than a sneaking suspicion that she already looked the part.

Hearing her enter despite the fact that he'd just turned on the blender, Andrew turned from the stove to look at his newest house guest. She'd brought the boy with her. And that instantly brought out a smile from him. ''Good morning.''

Suspending his spatula, he smiled down at the boy who was hanging onto her arm, looking back at him with wide, clear-blue eyes. Eyes that reminded him a great deal of Clay, he thought.

"And what's your name?"

If he thought that the boy might be shy, he was in for a surprise. All hints at possible shyness went out the window the second he opened his mouth.

"Alex," the boy announced with pride. He was clearly eyeing the profusion of toys even as he politely remained standing by his mother. "Is this your house?"

Andrew was taken aback by the boy's display of precocious behavior. At the very least, the child seemed as poised as one closer to the end of his first decade rather than just approaching the middle of it.

"Yes, it is," he told him, "and you and your mom are going to be staying here with me and my family for a little while." Out of the corner of his eye he saw Ilene shifting. He knew she was here unwillingly.

Alex couldn't contain himself any longer. "Whose toys are those?"

"Alex." Ilene gave her son a warning look, although she had to admit she was proud that the boy hadn't lunged at the toys yet.

Andrew held up his hand, stopping her from saying anything. "That's okay. They belonged to my kids when they were your age. I thought you might like playing with them."

Alex's head immediately whirled around in her direction. "Can I, Mama?"

That the man had gone to all this trouble for her child warmed her no end. "Since Mr. Cavanaugh was kind enough to get these out for you, yes, it'll be all right." She barely had time to finish her sentence when Alex dove into the bonanza.

Andrew nodded at the profusion on the rug. "I don't have any of those electronic video games, but—"

Ilene cut short the apology she saw coming. "He doesn't have any at home, not yet. I wanted him to develop his own imagination before he went on to harvest anyone else's."

Andrew studied her for a moment, deciding that he liked the woman a great deal. He couldn't help wondering why Clay had never mentioned her. She didn't strike him as the usual type his son went after. And that was a good thing.

"Sounds like a good plan to me." His eyes indicated the counter littered with various items in different stages of preparation. "Are you hungry?"

Her stomach felt as if it was tightly wrapped up with a cord. Hungry? She still wasn't sure she could eat. "I don't usually have breakfast."

Andrew believed the old adage about breakfast being the most important meal of the day. "Well, that's going to change, at least while you're here."

"Don't bully the woman, Dad. She can just have coffee if she wants."

Ilene turned and saw the blond police detective she'd met briefly in her home last night. But as the woman drew closer, Ilene found herself thinking that she looked a little younger than she'd first thought.

Hands occupied with separating bacon strips, Andrew nodded toward the blonde with his chin. "Ilene, Lorrayne. Rayne, Ilene."

Alex's dark head bobbed as he briefly glanced up from the middle of the light rug. "And I'm Alex."

Rayne crouched down beside him long enough to tousle his hair. "Hello, Alex, nice to meet you. You don't have to have breakfast, either."

Looking as if he was just short of salivating, Alex protested, "But I want breakfast."

"Then you can have it," Rayne told him with a quick, infectious grin as she rose to her feet.

Andrew nodded his head in approval. "I knew I liked you, boy, first time I saw you."

Alex cocked his head, his perfect brows drawing together over a perfect nose. "You mean just now?"

"No, last night." Andrew poured batter on the griddle. "I carried you from the car. You were sound asleep."

"It was past my bedtime," Alex informed him before returning to the flight pattern he'd established for the airplane he'd discovered.

Andrew chuckled to himself as he made eye contact with Ilene. "He's a pistol."

"That and more," Ilene agreed.

"Hi, what's for breakfast, I'm starved."

Turning toward the sound of the exuberant voice behind her, Ilene saw almost a carbon copy of the woman already in the room. But this time Ilene was fairly sure that the woman walking into the kitchen was the one she'd met last night.

Stealing a piece of crisp bacon that had come off a frying pan only seconds ago, the woman dropped down in a chair. "Carrying around dolls in the middle of the night always leaves me hungry."

Andrew gestured at the by now familiar array. He cooked like this daily, enjoying providing for a family that technically no longer needed him to continue providing. "French toast, pancakes, waffles, eggs, take your pick."

Ilene stared at him. She heard Rayne laugh and realized that she probably hadn't managed to mask her thought.

"Feels like you wandered into a restaurant, doesn't it?" Rayne asked.

Ilene looked at Andrew, unable to conceive of anyone doing anything this elaborate on a regular basis. "Please, don't go all out on our account."

"You've got nothing to do with it, trust me. Except that maybe he's put on a cleaner shirt in your honor. Dad's like this all the time, aren't you, Dad?"

The voice sounded as if it belonged to Clay, only deeper. But as she turned, she saw a tall, well-built man slipping into a chair at the table. She'd never seen a kitchen table quite as long as this one before. Lengthwise, it looked as if it had been lifted out of an army mess hall.

"So, how was your first night at the Cavanaugh Hilton?" the man who looked so distressingly like Clay asked. "Good, I hope."

She looked at him uncertainly, trying to get names straight. "Shaw?"

Shaw grinned, looking at Teri. "Not bad, she's got an eye for good-looking faces."

Rayne snorted. Of all of them, she was the one who most sounded like their father. "Don't flatter yourself, it's just a process of elimination. You're not Clay, so you're Shaw." She plopped down next to him. "She hasn't met the others."

Ilene looked at the long table again, quickly counting out the chairs that were still empty. "Others?" she echoed.

Teri nodded. "Dad likes to have everyone over for breakfast." She glanced fondly toward her father. "Claims it's his way of keeping tabs on us. On a good day, or bad, depending on which side of the bed you woke up—" she began to count off on her fingers— "he'll have all five of us here, plus Patrick and Patience, Janelle, Dax, Jared and Troy. And sometimes Uncle Brian."

That was thirteen. She noted that there were sixteen chairs, although not all at the table. Some were scattered throughout the family room, ready to be pressed into service if necessary. "Who are all those people?"

"Cousins," Rayne told her. "He lures them over with food. Man cooks better than an angel."

''Thank you,'' Andrew piped up.

''You're welcome. Keep cooking.'' Rayne leaned in confidentially toward Ilene. ''When he's busy cooking, he can't pry.''

''I heard that,'' Andrew told his youngest.

''As much,'' Rayne tacked on as an addendum for Ilene's benefit.

The whole scene took Ilene's breath away. It was hard for her to imagine having that many people over to attend a party, much less on any kind of a regular basis. How could Clay have such a warm, family-oriented father when he was such a devil-may-care bachelor? It didn't make sense to her.

The back door opened and closed. Behind her, she heard two more voices chorus a greeting. Turning, she saw three young men entering and recognized none of them.

Where was Clay? Why hadn't he come down yet, she wondered.

Returning his nephews' greetings, Andrew deposited his first batch of French toast onto a platter and glanced up to see the expression on Ilene's face. Taking pity on her, he rounded the counter and positioned himself so that his back was to his family.

''He's not here,'' he told Ilene.

Ilene flushed. Was she that transparent? ''I, um, wasn't—''

Wanting to spare her any further embarrassment, he cut her short. ''Clay went in early today. Said he wanted to see if that warning left at your house had any latent prints he could use.''

She nodded. Of course, that was what she wanted him to do. Find out who was doing this and make them stop. The feeling of abandonment refused to leave.

Andrew squeezed her hand. ''Feel like pitching in and helping an old man?''

She knew what he was doing and was grateful to him. In response, she forced a smile to her lips. It got easier. ''I would if I could find one.''

''You'll do, Ilene,'' Andrew pronounced with an approving nod of his head, ''you'll do. By the way,'' he began, turning so that he now faced the others, ''these strapping bulls-in-a-china-shop are my nephews Dax, Jared and Troy.'' He gestured toward each as he made the introduction. ''As a rule, they don't usually descend all together. Where's your sister, boys?''

Rayne laughed. ''Never enough for you, is it Pop?''

He ignored her, waiting for an answer from one of his nephews. He got it from the oldest, Dax.

''Janelle sends her regrets, but she had to go in early.''

''Patrick's not coming, by the way,'' Troy chimed in. ''And Patience had early surgery.''

''Patience is a doctor?'' Ilene asked as she followed Andrew back behind the stove.

"A vet," he corrected. "She always loved animals."

Now she remembered, Ilene thought, Clay had mentioned that to her yesterday.

"Unlike Clay, who always was an animal," Teri piped up. She took a head count around the table. "Speaking of whom, where is he?"

"Work," Andrew told her.

Shaw hooted. "Since when?" It wasn't that Clay was a poor detective, quite the opposite was true. But he wasn't exactly known for the long hours he put in. At least, not at the station.

So, this was different, then, Ilene thought. Clay was usually here in the morning. Had he deliberately changed his routine and gone in to work just to avoid her?

What if he had? Wasn't that what she'd wanted? she asked herself. To avoid him as much as possible? This was supposed to be a safe house, not a place where she could interact with the man who had refused to leave the site of her dreams no matter how hard she tried to evict him.

But if this was a good thing, why did she feel so adrift?

"You watch the bacon," Andrew told her. "I'll take care of the eggs." He looked around at the faces surrounding his table. "Okay, who wants eggs this morning and how do you want them?"

Rayne sighed. "Cholesterol, Pop, remember?"

"Eggs have been downgraded on the list, remember?'' he echoed her tone and looked back at the others. ''Now, again, who wants eggs?''

A show of hands appeared as the rear door opened and two more people entered. Greetings were tossed to Callie, Clay's oldest sister, and a man who finally did not resemble the other men in the room. A little girl stood between them.

Outsiders? Ilene wondered. Outsiders who obviously meant a great deal to Callie if she judged by the look on the other woman's face.

''This is Brent and his lovely daughter, Rachel, our newest additions,'' Andrew told her.

''Almost additions,'' Shaw put in. ''Still time to bail out, Brent. It's not too late.''

'''Fraid it is,'' Brent replied. ''I've given your sister a life sentence.''

The others groaned as Andrew explained to Ilene in a stage whisper, ''In case you haven't figured it out, Brent's a judge. Our first. C'mon, Alex, it's time for breakfast. You can sit by Rachel here. Rachel, make him feel at home,'' he instructed the little girl, who looked more than happy to undertake the task.

Ilene smiled to herself as she let Andrew usher her into a chair. She took solace in the banter and in pretending, just for a little while, that she fit into this large, loving group.

Even if Clay wasn't there.

Chapter 7

"We've got a match."

Adrenaline still throbbing through his veins from a taxing nonproductive meeting with John Walken, Clay looked up at the tall, thin police lab tech who came hurrying into the room. The man waved a piece of paper that was hot off the printer. Before he and Santini had left to see Walken, he'd given the tech the drawing of the three monkeys that had been taped to Ilene's dining room window. It was a long shot, but he'd hoped that the drawing would give them some kind of lead.

"Don't toy with me, Harry," Clay warned wearily. "I just spent the past hour talking to a guy who makes one of those oil tanker spills look like it came out of a bottle of bubble bath."

Clay knew from talking to Ilene that she thought Walken was an upstanding and, up until now, decent citizen who'd possibly just gotten caught up in something that had gone out of control. But he didn't see it that way. Walken struck him as a little too cool, a little too calculating. He was as certain that the man was behind the monkey drawing as he was that the sun was going to rise again tomorrow. And just as certain that things would escalate if Ilene didn't recant her findings. Ilene was far too innocent, never seeing the bad in people, always thinking they were good because she was.

Things hadn't changed all that much in six years, he thought. Ilene had had an innocence to her that he'd found incredibly attractive. She always assumed everyone and everything was good until shown otherwise.

He recalled the look on her face when they'd broken up. Well, he'd certainly shown her, hadn't he?

Annoyed that he was letting guilt get the better of him when it was far too late to do anything about it, he roused himself as he looked at Harry.

"So, what've you got?" he asked.

Harry Nagan smiled proudly. "Found one print where he pressed the tape down on the paper."

Rising, Clay slapped the tall, thin man on the back. "Knew you wouldn't let us down. Who's the print belong to?"

"Warren 'Weasel' Smith," Harry recited. Excited by his find, he'd printed up the felon's rap sheets and now handed them to Clay. "A small-time do-almost-anything-for-hire thug."

Santini clapped his hands together. "Yes, Virginia, there is a Santa Claus." Standing behind Clay, Santini read the particulars over his partner's shoulder.

The man was penny-ante, Clay thought, reading over his priors. "Weasel have a last-known address?"

"Right here." Taking liberty, Harry took back the extra papers and flipped to the last page. "Got it from his parole officer. 'Papa' Bill Anderson."

The parole officer, generally liked by the precinct personnel, had been at his job as long as anyone could remember. Married to it after three failed attempts at a regular union, he seemed to genuinely care about the men and women he saw on the other side of his desk.

Clay shook his head as he read through the report. "Wonder if Papa knows what junior is up to these days." He glanced again at the address before tossing the file on his desk. "Let's go."

Santini fell into place beside him. For a big man he moved as fast as someone half his size. "Think he'll still be there?"

That was the million-dollar question, Clay thought. "Maybe we'll get lucky."

It took them a little while to get lucky.

Their quarry wasn't at home when they went calling, but a twenty-dollar-spiked conversation with the superintendent, who was repairing a broken lock down the hall, gave them a new place to look. The superintendent told them he thought he'd seen Weasel frequenting the corner bar more than once. As Clay recalled, there'd been a drug bust there recently. Shanghai Pete's wasn't exactly a place known for its upscale clientele.

"We could get him for consorting with known criminals right off the bat and work our way up to something more binding," Santini suggested as they made their way out of the dilapidated building again.

Clay didn't answer. His stony expression was identical to the one he'd been wearing all day. Except for when the veins had stood out in his neck after the frustrating Walken interview. Exasperated at the silent treatment, Santini took the bull by the horns.

"Hey, what crawled up your butt and died today, Cavanaugh?" Clay gave him a steely look as he slipped behind the wheel. "You've been like a wounded bear all morning." Santini cocked his head, studying Clay's profile. "Some hot little number say no?"

He was in no mood to banter. "Get your own life, Santini. Stop trying to live vicariously in mine. Nobody said no, because nobody was asked."

"This about the case?"

Driving, Clay stared straight ahead. "Yes."

Santini paused. "About the woman in the case?"

Clay gave him a silencing look before turning back to the road. "You only get two questions a day, Santini, and you've already used them up." Though he was smiling, Clay's meaning was clear. "Save the others for our pal Weasel."

Santini sighed and shook his head.

The man behind the bar was neither cooperative nor friendly when Clay and Santini first walked in. But the owner who doubled as a bartender already had two violations issued against him by the city and wasn't looking to jam himself up any further with a third. So after a minimum of prodding and a flash of twin badges, the bartender pointed out a man sitting at the other end of the sticky bar.

As Clay began to approach him, Weasel bolted off his stool and tried to make a run for it. His goal was the back exit. He never made it. Santini blocked the path with his bulk alone.

Clay come up behind Weasel, amused by the expression on the suspect's face. Everyone looked stunned the first time they met Santini. He looked as if he belonged on some professional football team instead of the police department.

Taking hold of the back of the man's collar, Clay spun him around. "Looks like you just met the immovable object, Weasel. Mind if we call you Weasel?"

"It's better than Warren." His resentment vibrated in the air as the man mumbled into his non-existent chin.

Still holding him by his collar, Clay brought Weasel over to one of the three rickety tables that were spread about the dim bar and deposited him into a chair. He and Santini took chairs on either side of him, buffering Weasel with their bodies.

Looking like the poster boy for the cold and flu season, Weasel wiped his nose with the back of his discolored shirtsleeve. His eyes darted furtively from one detective to the other. He looked scared.

It could have been an occupational habit, Clay thought, but he doubted it.

''Whatever it is, I didn't do it.''

Clay's tone was deceptively genial. ''How do you know what we're going to ask?'' He pretended to sniff the air around Weasel. ''Maybe we're the hygiene police and we're here to ask if you took a shower this morning.''

Santini hooted as he made a face. Their suspect smelled of stale sweat, smoke and alcohol. And a few other scents that were best left unplaced. ''Pretty safe bet he didn't do that, either.''

Clay nodded, as if he was taking the answer into account. ''Okay.'' And then he pinned Weasel Smith with a sharp look. ''Did you leave a certain drawing taped on Ilene O'Hara's dining room window last night?''

Smith crossed his painfully thin arms before him

as if to protect his equally thin chest and muttered sullenly, "Don't know no Eileen O'Hara."

Clay worked hard at keeping his temper. They had this man dead to rights. Sometimes the game was hard to play.

"How about the address?" Clay rattled off Ilene's address. He got into Smith's face, trying not to think how frightened Ilene had looked when he'd arrived last night. "Does that ring a bell?"

Smith remained silent.

Santini inclined his head toward the man, holding his breath a little in self-defense. "I'd talk to him if I were you, Weasel. He's got the shortest temper in the squad room and you really don't want to see him once he gets going."

Their suspect looked genuinely frightened. His eyes darted toward the bartender, but if the latter was listening, he gave no indication of it. Smith's voice bordered on hysteria. "You're police. You can't do that. I could sue."

Clay's tone was low, quiet, and all the more chilling for it. "You'd have to be alive to sue, Weasel."

That was warning enough for the man. He hadn't been paid enough to die. "Yeah, I was there."

Clay drew his chair in closer. "Who put you up to it?"

"I don't know." Real fear entered the marble-like eyes.

Clay struggled to keep from grabbing Weasel by the shirt and shaking the answers loose out of him.

"Don't tell me. You just had a vision and drew these three monkeys, then went and taped them up on someone's house at random."

"No." He raked his dirty fingers through even dirtier, stringy hair. "I got a call from this guy." Unable to sit still, he'd been tapping his foot under the table. It began to sound as if a squadron of flamenco dancers had entered the bar. Clearly afraid, Smith looked from one detective to the other again. "The whole thing was done by phone. The guy said he wanted me to tape this on some woman's window, maybe scare her a little, rattle a few windows, try the door, that's all. He said it was a prank. Monkeys. What do I know?"

"Apparently very little," Santini commented.

"Go on," Clay urged angrily.

Smith rocked in his chair now as if preparing for a body blow. "He left the money for me at a drop-off point. I didn't see nobody, I swear."

"You recognize the voice?" Clay asked.

He knew the answer before Smith starting shaking his head. "No."

Exasperated, Clay sighed. Another dead end loomed before him and he was in no mood for it. "You always do business like this?"

One bony shoulder rose and fell in a hapless movement. "This way I can't finger anybody." Just the slightest hint of boldness came to the fore. "Can I go now?"

"Yeah, you can go." Closing his hand around

Smith's shirtfront, Clay rose, hauling the man up to his feet with him. "Go directly to jail. Do not pass go, do not collect two hundred dollars."

"But I told you everything I know," Smith protested frantically. "Taping a drawing up on a window isn't a crime."

Clay fell back on the charge his partner had originally come up with. "No, but consorting with known criminals is a parole violation. We figure maybe Papa Bill might want to talk to you, tell you how disappointed he is with you."

Defeated, Smith sighed as he allowed himself to be handcuffed and led out of the establishment.

Clay felt beat.

The rest of the day had been far less rewarding than their encounter with Smith. He and Santini had spent time combing through a month of Smith's telephone records. He'd requisitioned them the minute he'd gotten back to the office. Not that it really mattered. The call from whoever had paid Smith off to leave the drawing had come from a telephone booth.

It came as no surprise.

Santini had left the squad room more than half an hour ago, telling him to pack it in for the night and go home. "We can always go at stuff better after a good night's sleep," he'd said as he'd walked out.

Good night's sleep. That was a laugh. Clay sincerely doubted that that was in the cards for him tonight. Not as long as Ilene was under the same roof.

He flipped through the report Harry had left with him. There was absolutely nothing new there. He'd gone over it until the pages were worn. There was nothing more he could do tonight. He wanted to remain in the office.

Tired, edgy, with no new news, no headway, he just didn't feel up to facing Ilene. He had nothing to tell her that would help erase any of the fears he'd seen in her eyes last night. They couldn't pin this on Walken or any of the other CEOs, at least not yet.

But not assuaging her fears wasn't the only reason he didn't want to face her.

Over the course of the day he'd almost called her three times. Almost. But each time he'd flipped his cell phone closed, squelching the effort before it ever was completed.

The less contact he and Ilene had, the better off they'd both be.

Or so he told himself.

Rocking back in his chair, he blew out a breath. He knew he couldn't put off going home, especially not tonight. His father was throwing a party, one that actually had a reason for being this time. It was Rayne's twenty-fifth birthday, and he would catch hell from all sides if he didn't attend.

Clay closed his eyes. Ilene's image rose before him. Muttering a curse, he opened them again.

He was being a coward and he knew it. That didn't happen very often, and he hated the feeling that came with it. He'd never been a coward. Any time he dealt with fear, it just goaded him on—

That wasn't strictly true. He'd been a coward once before. And that time had involved Ilene, too.

With a sigh, he logged off his computer and shut it down.

When he turned onto his father's block, Clay noticed there was no place to park in the immediate area. Cars littered both sides of the street, almost nose to tailpipe. The vehicles, big and little, spilled over to the next block in both directions. Clay was forced to leave his own car several streets over.

As he walked back to the house, his hands shoved in his pockets, the fog from this morning had returned and now enshrouded him.

Somehow, it seemed fitting.

By the time he arrived at the front door, key in hand, his hair was iced with droplets of condensation. The cool, clammy air had seeped into his clothing. It did nothing to improve his mood.

The blast of hot air and noise that hit him the moment he unlocked the front door immediately began to evaporate both the droplets and his mood.

For a moment he just stood there, absorbing everything, trying to focus on who was where. Every place he looked, he saw another member of his fam-

ily. He tried hard not to zero in on Ilene. He succeeded.

But when he didn't see her immediately, he wondered if she'd been stubborn and taken off, going
back to her place. It would be just like her.

Just when he was about to turn around and take
a run over to her place, he saw her. She was walking
in from the kitchen, carrying a tray of one of those
concoctions that his father liked to make so much.
The parts Clay could readily identify involved
cheese and crackers, but there were a lot of other
things residing in the velvety spread he felt were
best left anonymous. Bottom line was that it tasted
good.

He supposed love was a little like that, too. There
were things you could identify and things that defied
classification. The bottom line was important there,
too.

What the hell was going on in his head? Had seeing her so suddenly after all this time thrown him
completely off-kilter?

He was determined not to let it.

Taking a breath, Clay deliberately made his way
over toward her. Time to take the bull by the horns,
to challenge himself to be a man and not a mouse.

Right now, being a mouse was beginning to have
its appeal.

His father was right behind Ilene, another tray of
the same origin in his hands. Any attempts at what

could have been an apology to Ilene died before it was born.

He frowned at his father. "I didn't leave her here to be pressed into service, Dad."

Andrew placed the tray on a table, then took the one Ilene was holding and put it down next to the first. "Then maybe you should have stuck around a little this morning and been a little more explicit in your instructions." To underscore his point, Andrew indicated Ilene with his eyes.

His father was telling him he shouldn't have left Ilene like that the first morning she was here. But this wasn't a social thing; it was professional. And as a professional, he didn't have time to baby-sit a woman he'd covertly forced to break up with him because he hadn't had the nerve to make a commitment.

"I don't mind," Ilene told him. The look on Clay's face told her he didn't believe her. "Helping out keeps me from going stir-crazy." She glanced at Andrew and smiled. "Besides, I like pitching in."

"I can always use another pair of hands," Andrew affirmed. He looked over to the side where he had Alex and Rachel folding napkins just to make the two feel part of the whole. The two children seemed to be getting along very well. He looked back at Clay. "Since you're here, why don't you go in and bring out your sister's cake?" With a nod of his head, Clay began to head for the kitchen. "Don't drop it," Andrew called after him.

Clay rolled his eyes as he kept walking. "I'm not ten, Dad."

"No, you're not," Andrew agreed. "What you are is clumsy."

Clay stopped dead and turned around. He held up one finger. "Once, I dropped something once," he reminded his father.

"It happens once, it can happen again."

"Make sure there's no cat to trip over and it won't," Clay said over his shoulder as he made his way into the kitchen.

He found Rayne there, dipping her finger into the whipped chocolate icing. She raised her eyes when she saw him walking in. A lop-sided grin lit her face.

"Busted."

He laughed. "Hi, kid, happy birthday."

Rayne raised her chin. "I'm not a kid anymore. I'm twenty-five."

"And I'm two years older. To me, you'll always be a kid." He moved the huge sheet cake closer before he picked it up. "Someday that'll be a comfort."

Rayne frowned as she stuck her hands into her back pockets. "Maybe, but right now, it's a pain in the butt, always being the baby."

He laughed, pausing to give his sister a one-arm hug. "Like you were *ever* a baby. You were born old, Rayne. And then you made Dad that way."

Her eyes took on the same twinkle he'd seen in

his father's. The two were more alike than either wanted to admit.

"It's a damn dirty job, but someone had to do it," she cracked.

Ilene stuck her head in the doorway in time to catch the exchange. Seeing him with his family was showing her a side to Clay she had no idea existed. He could be warm and loving under the right conditions. The conditions just hadn't included her, she thought ruefully. At least, not for long.

"Need any help?" she offered.

"I've got it under control," Clay told her. He picked up the heavy cake. It could probably be a meal all by itself, if you were given to eating sweets exclusively, he thought. "But you can handle the candles and the matches if you want." He nodded at the items on the table.

Ilene picked up the box of small blue candles, Rayne's favorite color, and the book of matches that only saw use at birthdays and followed Clay and his sister back into the living room.

Clay placed the cake in front of his father, who always did the honors. He stepped back, nearly stepping on Ilene's toes. She shifted to the side just in time.

"Where were you all day?" she asked in a hushed voice as everyone gathered around to watch Andrew begin the process of lighting the candles.

Clay stared straight ahead, trying not to inhale the perfume she always wore. Trying not to want the woman who was wearing it. "Trying to find out who left that drawing at your place."

Ilene held her breath as she looked at him. She wanted the path to lead to someone other than her boss. And she wanted this to be over. "And did you?"

"Yes."

She swallowed. She felt her heart begin to hammer again. "Do I know him?"

He looked at her then and saw the disappointment that came into her eyes when he said, "No."

"I don't understand. Then why—"

She was in denial, he thought. He guessed he could see it from her point of view. She didn't want to believe that someone she knew would want to hurt her. "He was hired by someone. It's just as we thought, they did it to scare you off."

She braced her shoulders and he knew that the attempt had failed. Walken, or whoever was responsible, might have wanted to scare Ilene off, but all they had done was get her to dig in.

Part of Clay was proud of her, part of him wanted to convince her that it just wasn't worth the risk.

But the lights were being dimmed just then. His father cleared his throat and led the gathering in the traditional birthday song. It was sung very much off-key despite the fact that several of them could actually carry a tune.

Singing along, Clay decided to table any further discussion until later.

Chapter 8

The singing died down amid groans proclaiming this to be the worst rendition of "Happy Birthday" ever. Rayne leaned over the center of the large sheet cake decorated with a cartoon version of a tough-as-nails policewoman dragging a criminal off to jail, made her wish and blew. The candles flickered valiantly, then died.

"Told you she was a windbag," someone joked.

Standing beside his youngest born, Andrew raised his hands, motioning for everyone to quiet down.

When they did, he said, "And now, ladies and gentlemen, or whatever you all call yourselves, I give you the baby of the family, Lorrayne Rose Cavanaugh." Glancing at her with pride, he saw the glare. "And don't give me that look, Rayne. Even if you're 125, you'll always be the baby of the family.'' His blue-gray eyes took measure of his children. ''Face it, you're not getting off the hook until one of these sluggards you call your brothers and sisters decides to do the right thing, get married and give me that first grandchild.''

Clay laughed along with the others. It was a familiar refrain that still managed to tickle everyone, especially when it got under Rayne's skin.

Glancing toward Ilene to see if she shared in the humor, he noticed that she was looking at Alex just as his father had mentioned getting his first grandchild. There was something about the look that gave him pause.

He knew what he'd said to his father when the latter had raised the subject to him last night—that Alex wasn't his. Couldn't be his. He'd been so sure when he'd said it. The timing was off, and besides, he felt certain that Ilene would have told him if the boy was his.

At least, fairly certain, anyway.

Even so, he felt his pride sting. The time line excluded him as father, but it did indicate that the second he and Ilene had broken up, she had found someone else to replace him.

Maybe even before they'd broken up.

He looked at her now as she drew her son to her, laughing at something Callie said to her. A restless, unsettled feeling grew within him.

Had he been that easy to get over? That easy to forget?

Damn it, what was the matter with him? What was he doing, being jealous of hypothetical situations that might or might not have been true? Situations revolving around a woman he had willingly walked away from?

For reasons that now looked incredibly threadbare to him, he thought, as he watched her help Rayne slice the cake and hand it out.

"Hey, cuz, what's up?" Dax, his uncle Brian's oldest son, came up next to him and slapped a hand on his shoulder. "You look like you're a million miles away in not so pretty territory."

Clay shook his head. Close to all his cousins, he didn't feel like going into anything right now. This was something he needed to figure out for himself. "Just thinking about the case I'm working on."

Dax pretended to take a step back as he stared at his younger cousin. "God, you *have* grown up, haven't you, Clay? Time was, when you'd be thinking about the latest lady you were working on, not a case."

Why did that sound so shallow to him? It had been acceptable enough just a few days ago. Or had it? Maybe that was where this restlessness came from. He'd grown dissatisfied with the way his life was going—nowhere.

Taking a breath, he shrugged. "Yeah, well, we've all got to grow up sometime."

There was a contrary grin on Dax's face. Of all of the male members of the family, Dax had the wildest reputation when it came to women. The standing family joke was that Dax had never met a woman he didn't like.

"Not me. I'm staying 'charmingly boyish—'" he winked at Clay, using terminology Clay guessed someone had applied to him "—until they bury me at eighty or so with a very satisfied grin on my face."

Clay might have willingly followed such a credo once, but it seemed very hollow to him right now. Not wanting to get maudlin, Clay raised the glass of champagne his father had made certain everyone had just before they began singing and toasted his cousin. "More power to you, Dax."

Clay heard his father's voice above the others. "Ah, Clay, you want to make a toast?" Turning, he saw the look on the man's face. Obviously, his raised glass had caught his father's eye.

He played along willingly. "Yeah, I do. To my baby sister," Clay began, and laughed as he saw the face that Rayne made at him. "Took a long time, but you're finally almost bearable. Keep up the good work." In response, Rayne stuck her tongue out at him. "Uh-oh, looks like we've had a momentary lapse back to the old Rayne." He ducked as she feigned throwing his piece of the cake at him.

Ilene had just eased the slice onto a plate. So this was what it was like, she thought longingly. This was what it felt like, sounded like to have a family gathered around you, a family that really cared about you and wasn't just marking time until you were old enough to move on with your life, a life away from theirs. She couldn't help feeling envious of Clay.

Regret wafted through her. She stopped what she was doing, letting Andrew continue doling out the slices that Rayne cut.

"Anything wrong, girl?" Andrew whispered.

Ilene realized tears had gathered in her eyes and that the man had seen them. Fighting embarrassment, she blinked a couple of times, but that only succeeded in causing one of the tears to slide down her face.

"No, nothing," she told him, accepting the handkerchief he offered her. "I always get sentimental at birthdays."

Taking the handkerchief back and tucking it into his pocket, he pretended to believe her. "Well then, if you were part of this family, I'd say you'd be in for a lot of crying."

There were worse things. She smiled at his comment. "I could handle it."

His eyes were kind, crinkling. "I bet you could at that."

Clay watched the exchange, though he couldn't hear anything that was being said. He had a hunch he knew, though. His father was getting way too cozy with Ilene. Undoubtedly, he was pumping her for information. The man had a way of extracting things from people without their knowing. It was a gift he'd honed as a detective and one that had pretty much been perfected at home.

Time to separate them, Clay decided, making his way through the crowd. When he reached her, Ilene mechanically handed him a piece of cake. Clay took it, even though the last thing on his mind was eating.

"What does he want you to do now?" Clay asked, looking at his father accusingly.

"Have a good time," Andrew replied, then gave his younger son a penetrating look. The one designed to make the recipient feel underage. "Since when did you get so suspicious?"

"Since I found out how sneaky you could be. Basically, from about the age of two and beyond. C'mon, Ilene." He took the plate she was holding out of her hand and placed it on the buffet table, "I'll introduce you around."

Hesitating, Ilene glanced over toward where her son was. Alex still played with his new-found best friend, Rachel. Callie and Rachel's father, Brent, were sitting beside them, apparently enjoying the children's interaction.

For a second, looking quickly, Ilene thought that could have been her and Clay instead of his sister and her fiancé. Her hair was a little darker than Callie's strawberry-blond and Brent's a little lighter than Clay's black hair, but it could have been them. Should have been them. She felt her heart ache.

If wishes were horses, beggars would ride.

Wasn't that something her mother had said to her on more than one occasion? It usually came at the end of a crying jag that followed a blowup between her parents. Her mother would look at her and declare how she wished her life had turned out differently. And Ilene always knew what she meant. That her mother wished she hadn't given in to pressure and gotten married just to give her daughter a legal name.

Forced marriages never worked out. For anyone involved.

"I'm surprised," Ilene murmured as he drew her over to a cluster of people she'd already met that morning. "You never wanted to introduce me to anyone in your family when we knew each other."

The phrasing she used caught his attention. When they knew each other. Meaning they no longer did. Well, it was true, wasn't it? They didn't know each other anymore. Why did that bring such a pang to him?

About to approach a group of his cousins, Clay paused. "I thought you wanted to keep it simple," he reminded her. It was an excuse for his actions, nothing more. Seeing her now, he knew he should have handled things differently then.

"I did," she lied.

The lie grew more elaborate, gaining depth and breadth.

"Well, this crowd is anything but simple. Hell, I always felt as if I was part of a small town whenever

Dad had them all over for some occasion or other. Like breakfast.'' He laughed.

He hadn't introduced her to anyone then not to spare her, or play along with any sort of simplicity requirement on her part, he hadn't introduced her because he hadn't wanted her getting entrenched in his family. Hadn't wanted them accepting her and silently and not-so-silently goading him on to the next step. A step he wasn't prepared to take.

Because when you loved someone and they left your life, you never recovered. His dad had taught him that. Not in any words, but he only had to look into his father's eyes to know it was true.

"Well, I think it's nice."

He was about to say something flip about the grass always being greener, but then relented. She was right. He wouldn't have traded his family for anything. Ever.

"Yeah, well maybe it is," he acknowledged in an offhanded manner. Taking her arm, he drew her over to two of what his father referred to as Brian's boys. "Anyway, over here's—"

"Dax and Troy," she told him. "Yes, I know. Save yourself some trouble, Clay, I met them at breakfast. Met most of them at breakfast," she added. "As a matter of fact, the only one who seemed to be missing at breakfast was you."

Though she tried not to let it, a part of her was hurt that Clay had just abandoned her like that this morning, going off without so much as a word. You would have thought she'd have learned by now, Ilene thought. She certainly had enough to go on as to his MO. There were no promises as far as Clay was concerned. That way they could never be broken.

Only her heart could be.

He noticed the way Dax was looking at her. Something territorial arose within Clay. He moved and blocked her with his body. "I was busy trying to follow up a lead."

She nodded, looking away. Knowing that being so close to him like this was not the wisest thing she could do. Even though there was a crowd around, it didn't stop the desire that insisted on raising its head within her. "So your father said."

"Here, if you have to listen to him, don't do it on an empty stomach." Andrew seem to materialize out of nowhere, a plate with birthday cake in his hands. He pressed it on her.

"How could it be empty? There's food everywhere I look," Ilene pointed out.

"Which you hardly touched," Andrew countered.

Once the party had gotten underway, she hadn't eaten anything. But she could have sworn Andrew had been too busy to notice. "How did you—"

Clay cut off her protest. "Don't waste your breath, Ilene, the man is all-seeing. I learned that a long time ago. Most parents have eyes in back of their heads. Dad has eyes all over, like a fly."

Gray eyebrows drew over his nose as he regarded

his second son. "With that golden tongue of yours, I'm beginning to understand why you couldn't hang on to a good woman."

The remark caught her by surprise. Ilene looked at Andrew. Did he mean her? Or was that just a general, throwaway comment he was making about his son's way of life?

"Maybe the good woman didn't want to be hung on to," Teri suggested, coming up behind him.

They were ganging up on him. Normally, that didn't faze him. Tonight, however, there was something different going on. He didn't know if it was a simple matter of coming face-to-face with a portion of his past he had never felt right about, or something more. In any event, he wanted a chance to regroup.

Taking the cake from her, Clay popped the last piece into his mouth, then set the plate on the arm of the sofa. Andrew gave him a reproving look as he picked the plate up again.

"Want to get some air?" Clay suggested.

He obviously wanted to get away from his father and sister. But she didn't welcome the idea of being alone with him. Mainly because she wanted to be and she knew that was a dangerous road to walk.

"It's kind of chilly outside." It was her last line of defense.

"I can keep you warm," he volunteered.

"Yes, I know."

He'd meant by giving her a sweater, but then realized how it had come out. He tried again. "I want to talk to you."

About the man who'd frightened her last night? About the case? About the past? She wasn't going to find out playing guessing games in her head. "Okay."

"Holler if you need help," Andrew called after her.

She thought Clay's father was more than half-serious. He was a darling man, she thought. Clay didn't know how lucky he was.

His hand on her shoulder, Clay guided her through the throng of friends and relations until he reached the rear of the family room. Opening the patio door, he ushered her out, then slid the door closed behind them.

They were the only ones outside. A quarter moon shone above them.

Behind them, the volume of the sound had only gone down a little more than a notch. Clay noted it with a grin. "Dad had new windows and doors put in about a year ago. The salesman swore they'd mute the noise, but then, I guess we can't be too hard on him. He'd never encountered the Cavanaugh tribe."

There was affection in his voice even as he pretended to deride them. She tried not to let it seduce her. "You said you wanted to talk to me."

He shoved his hands into his pockets to keep from

sweeping her into his arms. "Cut right to the chase, right?"

Go back inside, she told herself. Inside's safer.

"I just don't want to seem rude to your father." It was a lie. Andrew Cavanaugh was the furthest thing from her mind right now. And Clay's lips were the closest as she tried to recall the feel of them against hers.

He studied her for a moment before saying anything. "Is it that? Or is it just that you don't want to be alone with me?"

"That has nothing to do with it."

She realized that she hadn't denied his allegation, she'd twisted it. Because she *was* afraid to be alone with him. Afraid of her own vulnerability, her own weakness. Afraid of the desire that ricocheted through her.

"Doesn't it?" That old longing slipped over him, the one that had prompted him to kiss her that very first time, in the quad, in the rain, while students all around them ran for shelter from the sudden spring downpour. Nothing had seemed quite as important as kissing her. Nothing did now.

She purposely stiffened her spine, praying the physical act would trigger an emotional one and make her shut down. It didn't.

"I'm not afraid of being alone with you, Clay. I got over you a long time ago. Just like you got over me."

His eyes held hers. "What makes you think I ever

got over you?'' He saw the momentary surprise flicker in her eyes before she banked it down. ''After all, you were the one to dump me.''

She was too smart to have been taken in by that. He'd used it as an excuse, a last-minute stay from the governor. ''Technically.''

''Still felt as if you dumped me,'' he insisted. ''I felt very dumped.''

Did he think she was that naive? They both knew he'd orchestrated it. ''And relieved, I'm sure.''

''Relieved?''

''You're not the type to be tied down. You told me so the very first time we met.'' She laughed softly, though her smile never touched her eyes. Or her soul. ''It was like having to read the disclaimer on a package I was unwrapping.''

''No packages were unwrapped until at least the third date.'' Restraining himself even that long had been hell. Just as it was now. He'd wanted her with every fiber of his being from the very first time he'd kissed her. Before. And like a man whose destiny had already been preordained, he felt himself being reeled in. Very slowly he ran his fingertips along the hollow of her throat. Mesmerizing himself.

''Don't,'' Ilene breathed, barely able to get the word out. Pinpricks of anticipation began to dance along her skin, quickening her loins, making her heart go into overdrive.

''Don't what?'' He felt excitement taking hold. ''Do you remember the first time I kissed you?''

"It was in the quad." The words came out of her lips in slow motion as the world around her froze, then slipped into shadow. She couldn't draw her eyes away from his. "It was monsooning. I caught a cold."

"So did I. It was worth it," he whispered just before his lips touched hers.

No, no, this wasn't happening. She wasn't going to let this happen. Wasn't going to buy a ticket for a ride on a roller coaster that would be over too soon. So why was she leaning into the kiss? Into him? Why had her entire system just gone haywire with an excitement that had been missing from her life for the past six long years?

She knew she should be trying to save herself.

And maybe she was. By staying just where she was.

Clay had missed her so much, missed this head-over-heels feeling, this rush that captured him the second he knew he was going to kiss her.

The second he did.

No other woman had ever done this to him. Made him want her beyond all reason. Because wanting her went beyond reason. He knew that. That was why he'd left in the first place.

She still had the power to scare the hell out of him, because there was this feeling that every shred of control over his own life could easily slip through his fingers, plummeting him into a place with smooth, shiny walls that couldn't be scaled.

A place he couldn't climb out of.

Okay, he knew that—knew the dangers, knew he couldn't linger here beyond the moment. Just the moment.

Just one very long, wonderful moment.

His hands left her face and slid to her shoulders, anchoring her in place. Anchoring him. Holding on to her so she could travel the distance with him. Just this one more time.

The kiss deepened, pulling him into the center of it with a force beyond the powers of nature. He willed time to stand still.

Ilene stopped short of threading her arms around his neck the way she so desperately wanted to. Stopped short when she felt her body cleaving to his, as if it had been created for just that purpose. Her heart hammering like the tap shoes of someone dancing an Irish jig, she drew back.

She was breathless, with possibly no prayer of ever catching her breath again. "That can't happen again," she told him.

"Why?"

Shaky, afraid of giving in to the temptation shimmering before her, Ilene took more than a few steps back. Away from him. She didn't have the luxury of being able to give in to him. To herself.

"Because I'm not twenty-one anymore. Because there's more than just me to think about now. I've got someone else depending on me, Clay, and Alex comes first. He always will."

He wanted to touch her again. To take her into his arms and just hold her, breathe in the scent of her hair. But the look in her eyes stopped him. Feeling almost rebellious, he shoved his hands into his back pockets.

"I'm not looking to replace Alex."

She felt like screaming, like crying. With supreme control, she held herself in check. "No, you're not looking for anything but a good time, just as you always have. I can't give it to you, Clay."

"I think you really underestimate yourself," he said. Unable to help himself, he feathered her silky hair through his fingers.

She raised her chin. "No, I'm just not willing to sell myself short anymore." She reached for the sliding glass door, pulling it open. "If you're through 'talking' to me, I'd better go back inside. Alex might be looking for me."

"No, I'm not through talking." His hand over hers, he slid the door shut again.

And then he asked the question she'd been dreading all along. The question that had haunted her mind and conscience since the moment the nurse had told her there was a life growing inside of her.

"Is Alex mine?"

Chapter 9

It took her a moment to find her tongue. Her voice was deadly still as she answered his question with a question. She prayed that her expression wasn't giving her away. "What makes you ask?"

"His coloring, for one. Alex looks a lot like my brother Shaw did at his age. The way you looked at him when my father was talking about getting his first grandchild, for another." His eyes held hers, looking for answers, finding none. "Maybe just a gut feeling."

Ilene grabbed on to the only thing she could honestly respond to. "Your gut feelings only work when you apply them to your job."

The breeze picked up. He shifted, blocking it from her with his body and creating a cozy alcove for the two of them. Maybe too cozy.

"This is an exception."

She looked at Clay, so tempted to tell him the truth that she ached. But she knew that it would have been weak of her to admit that Alex was his son, just as it would have been back when she'd discovered she was pregnant. Once he knew, Clay would do the right thing and it would turn out all wrong. And he'd wind up resenting her and Alex, if not actually hating them. She already knew how that scenario played itself out.

Maybe she would have felt differently if, just once, he had told her he loved her. But he hadn't, and anything said after the fact wouldn't ring true to her.

Ilene looked him straight in the eye. And lied. "It's also wrong."

He kept thinking that if he continued to look into her eyes, he could discern if she was telling him the truth. And yet, there was something that nagged at him, something that didn't feel right even when she didn't flinch, didn't look away.

"He's not mine." The words were almost a challenge.

"He's not yours."

He believed her and yet he didn't. She'd never lied to him or at least he'd never caught her in a lie, and yet...

"What's his father's name?"

Slowly she shook her head. Eye contact remained, although she wasn't sure how much longer she could maintain it, how much longer she could tough it out. "Sorry, but that's privileged information and I can't give it to you."

His eyes narrowed. "What is he, the president?"

"No." Her manner was cool, collected. Inside, her heart hammered like a continuous drumroll. "Just someone who wouldn't want his name bandied about." It was her turn to pin him with a look. "Put yourself in his position."

"I am." In more ways than you can guess, Clay thought.

She could almost read his mind. "Not that far into his position," she told him, opening the door to insure her getaway. "Just enough to be sympathetic."

She left him standing in the cold, looking in. Wondering.

Andrew turned from the garbage pail in the kitchen in time to see Ilene approaching with an armload of dinner plates. He moved to take them from her, but she sidestepped him, placing the stack on the counter. He shook his head. "You don't have to do this, you know."

"I know," she replied. Less than twenty-four hours in the man's company and she felt closer to him than she had after a lifetime with her father. "I want to."

"I have enough hands to help with cleanup," Andrew protested as Teri made her way in behind Ilene. "All I have to do is bully them into it."

Ilene began to rinse off the plates before putting them in the dishwasher. "You don't have to bully me, and I like doing it." She looked at him. "I *need* to be doing it."

Andrew gave her a knowing look. He'd felt the same need for the past fifteen years, trying to stay one step ahead of the thoughts that haunted him. "If you stay in perpetual motion, you don't have to think, is that it?"

She paused to look at him. "That's it."

Andrew nodded as he handed her a towel to dry off her hands. "Tell you what, Clay said something about you being an auditor?"

And had she been anything else, she wouldn't have been in this predicament. Ilene took a breath. "That's right, I am."

He cocked his head, studying her. "Does that mean you can untangle taxes?"

Doing income taxes had never held that dread she knew most people experienced. She'd always been good with numbers, always liked math. "For the most part."

Andrew cocked an eyebrow. "Really tangled-up taxes?"

She tried not to laugh. "Just how big a knot are we talking about?"

The shrug was noncommittal. "I kind of let things slide this year."

Her attention was captured. Helping Andrew was

the least she could do in exchange for his hospitality. "Did you file for an extension?"

"Yes." Andrew frowned. "And it's breathing down my neck. I'm supposed to have it done by the end of the year."

Which was quickly approaching, Ilene thought. It never ceased to amaze her how much people could procrastinate. She usually had her own taxes in order the moment all her necessary papers arrived in the mail, certainly no later than the beginning of February. She couldn't understand how people who waited until the last minute managed to get a decent night's sleep.

"He won't go to a tax consultant—" Clay told her as he walked into the kitchen with a bulging garbage bag filled with empty beer bottles and cans.

A firm believer in privacy, his father snorted. "None of their damn business what I've got. Bad enough I have to bare all to the government, I'm not about to go to some stranger with all my worldly goods done up in little pieces of paper."

Ilene looked at him. "But you're willing to trust me?"

There was no hesitation on Andrew's part. After thirty years on the force, he considered himself an excellent judge of character, and he liked what he saw in this woman. "Yes."

"I'm honored." A smile slowly curved Ilene's lips.

The shrug was quick, dismissive. "You've got an honest face."

"Apparently the only one around," Rayne cracked with a deep chuckle. Then she looked at Ilene a tad uneasily. "No offense."

"None taken," Ilene assured her.

Andrew waved a hand at the guest of honor. He was on a mission of mercy now. "Don't pay attention to her. Will you do it?"

She had a feeling that she and Alex were going to be here for at least a few days, which was longer than she would have liked. But if it couldn't be helped, she wanted to keep busy instead of counting tiles in the bathroom. "I'd be more than happy to take a look at it for you."

Coming back from where he'd dumped the trash into the recycle bin, Clay caught the tail end of the exchange. He shook his head. "You'll be getting into a lot."

"The more tangled, the better," she told him, and she meant it. "I'll get to it right after I drop off Alex at school and see Janelle."

"Back up," Clay said sharply. His tone caught her off guard, he could tell by the surprised look on her face. "What do you mean right after you drop Alex off at school? Alex isn't going anywhere."

She didn't like his tone. Hers became steely. "I thought part of the reason I'm staying here is so that Alex doesn't feel entirely uprooted."

Clay exchanged looks with his father. The woman

was incredibly naive. He thought the danger would have sunk in by now. There were bad guys after her and they wouldn't hesitate to use her son to get what they wanted. "And part of the reason is so that Alex doesn't get harmed if they want to up the ante on this. Ilene, I don't have the manpower to guard your son while he's attending preschool."

"He goes to a private school. They have a security system in place—"

Yeah, he'd just bet. Didn't she get it yet? "Anyone clever enough to hoodwink a large body of shareholders can easily circumvent the security system employed by a preschool—" he anticipated her protest "—fancy or not. Now unless you have enough money to hire the kid a personal bodyguard who's going to make Alex feel as if he's sticking out like a sore thumb because there's this adult standing around in his class, I suggest you forget about dropping him off anywhere tomorrow except the living room."

She was having a hard time with this. Andrew's heart went out to the woman. "I could ask one of my buddies to do a little private duty," he told her. "As a favor to me."

Clay was well aware of how the network of law enforcement agents within Aurora worked. It was a small, tight-knit community that looked out for one another. Still, he didn't like the idea of leaving Alex exposed, special detail or no special detail. Something could always go wrong, and the more risks that were taken, the more that could go wrong.

Clay glanced at Ilene before turning to his father. "The kid's taken to you, Dad. Why don't you just take Alex under your wing tomorrow and teach him how to cook, you know, something simple? It'll be different and it's something he can use once he's on his own." He turned his attention back to Ilene. "Bottom line is to keep him safe."

She blew out a breath. He was right and she knew it. She'd been thinking with her heart and not her head. "I just don't want to do anything that'll make him feel afraid." Once that seed was instilled, it could never be completely removed. And Alex was so fearless now, so happy. She didn't want anything to change that quality. Taking him away from everything he knew would accomplish that.

Clay pretended to take her words at face value. "Well, yeah, Dad can be scary at times, but he'll be on his best behavior, right, Dad?"

Putting away the little that was left of the two huge spiral hams he'd prepared, Andrew snorted. "Listen to him, you'd think he was treated with anything but kid gloves since the day he came into the world, hollering and screaming."

Clay picked at one of the leftover canapés. "If I was hollering and screaming, it was because I knew you were going to be my dad."

Another time she would have let herself be distracted by the banter. But not now. Not when this was being driven home to her. She had taken a step that would forever change her life, forever change Alex's life. Just like the step she'd taken six years ago.

She sighed, surrendering. "Okay."

Andrew immediately caught her drift. "Hey, it won't be so bad. Alex'll have fun," he promised. "And I've already talked to Brent about having Rachel dropped off here after school." He winked at Ilene. "I think Alex's got his first major crush."

He was a dear, dear man to have taken that upon himself, she thought. As for her son's infatuation with Rachel, she'd noticed it, too. A bittersweet pang drifted through her. "I know. I was hoping it'd be a few more years before I was replaced."

Andrew patted her hand. "Nobody replaces a mother in a boy's heart. She represents the first relationship he has with a woman, laying the foundation for all the others."

That was a little more philosophy than Ilene thought even her precocious son was capable of. About to laugh off the notion, Ilene saw the expression on Clay's face.

His father's words had struck a chord.

Maybe Andrew wasn't just trying to be nice to her. Maybe there was more than a little bit of truth in Andrew's words, she thought. Clay's mother had left him. Willingly or otherwise, she had left. Fear of abandonment could have gone a long way to making Clay think twice before forging another relationship with a woman.

The next moment she was rejecting her own theory. She was making excuses for Clay because she wanted to tell him that Alex was his. All these years, not a day went by when her secret hadn't weighed heavily on her conscience.

Doing the right thing wasn't always easy, she reminded herself. But keeping her secret was still the right thing to do.

"Damn it, she couldn't have just disappeared into thin air."

John Walken's angry voice echoed about the massive room where he retreated to be alone with his thoughts. His thoughts were now as dark as the rich, teak bookcases that comprised three of the four walls. Behind him on one wall a movie ran unnoticed, its image scattered along the fifty-inch plasma screen. He had all the toys, all the trappings of wealth a man could possibly want.

His toys were in jeopardy and he wouldn't stand for it.

"The next time you call, I want to hear that you found her, understand?" He didn't have to tack on a threat, it was understood.

The man on the other end of the line was quiet for a moment. His voice was strained with unreleased anger. "It's not like we're not trying."

Walken held up his brandy glass. The handsome

face reflected there was cold, deadly. "Try harder. The D.A.'s office just served me with papers for an indictment hearing."

That smug little Cavanaugh bitch had come to do it personally. Everywhere he turned, he felt as if the walls were closing in on him, on the life he'd fought so hard to forge. All because of one do-gooder he hadn't been able to control.

Control took on many forms, and he was ready to exercise the ultimate one.

Provided she was found in time.

The man on the other end attempted to reason with him. There was a great deal at stake. None of them could afford to lose their cool.

"It's just a fishing expedition. They can't prove anything. You've erased all the data from the hard drive, and we've substituted another computer for the one O'Hara was using," he reminded Walken. "There's no way they can get their hands on any substantiating data."

"Unless they have O'Hara. Damn it, this comes under the heading of protection. Something you've been more than happy to accept money for. Now protect me!"

"Her computer's the important thing, and that's history."

Rage bubbled in his veins and threatened to explode. "You don't think she's made copies? The woman's not an idiot, she knew no one was going to just take her word for anything. And you just told me your people didn't find anything at her house. That means she's got the damn laptop with her. I want it and her and the sooner the better.'' He took a breath, issuing the final threat. ''If I go down for this, I'm not going down by myself. You remember that.''

There was silence on the other end. ''I'll find her,'' the man promised. ''And when I do—''

Walken quickly interrupted the other man. He wanted no verbal exchange to actually implicate him. Even though things were understood. ''I want you to do whatever you have to do in order to fix the problem—and I don't want to know any details, other than the fact that this won't somehow come back and bite me on the butt.''

The other man's voice was condescending. Walken hated him, hated dealing with him, but he was a necessary evil. He'd never dreamed when he'd begun juggling things to come out in the black that it would lead him down this slippery slope. ''Consider it done.''

''It better be—before we are.'' Not waiting for anything further, Walken slammed down the receiver. He threw back the rest of the brandy, then poured himself another.

Giving up, Ilene threw off her covers and got out of bed. It was a little past midnight. She couldn't sleep. Clay had stirred up things within her so badly she felt as if someone had left a blender on inside. A blender with a broken switch.

Combing her fingers through her hair, she looked ruefully at her rumpled bed where she had tossed and turned for the past hour. She was exhausted, but there was no way she was going to get any sleep, at least not for a while.

Her laptop sat on the bureau. Might as well do something productive, she thought.

She switched on the main light and then took her laptop and placed it on the small desk where Callie had sat before her, doing her homework and complaining bitterly about the useless information she was required to learn. Andrew had told her that little tidbit when he'd settled her into this room earlier. Instead of downstairs, she was in an upstairs bedroom now, one that was connected to her son's room via a bathroom. Andrew had told her he thought she could use more space.

Sitting down, she smiled to herself. The man was going out of his way to make her feel welcomed, to make her feel a part of things, and she was more grateful to him than she could say.

But having Clay around made her feel hopelessly adrift, as if the past and the present had collided. For the first time in five years, she didn't have a game plan.

Other than surviving this ordeal and remaining as intact as she could manage.

Turning the computer on, she watched the screen

turn light, then dark, then light again as it went through the various stages of its wake-up cycle. The fan made a rattling noise for the first few minutes before settling down.

She keyed in a familiar code and pulled up the files she'd copied from her computer at work. She'd covertly transferred the files less than a week ago. It was against the rules, but then, so was embezzling, or whatever it was that John Walken chose to call what he'd done with Simplicity's funds.

One by one she carefully copied the files again, this time onto disks. Though her computer had never given her any trouble, she wasn't about to take chances. She was a firm believer in backing up files, especially in this case. The process was tedious. There was no CD burner attached to her laptop so she was relegated to copying the files onto disks. As they downloaded, she looked around the room, trying to find a safe place to hide the disks. What better place than in a house filled with police personnel?

She tried not to allow her thoughts to go anywhere beyond the parameters of the room.

Even so, as she sat, waiting, she ran her tongue along her lips.

Tasting him.

Or maybe she was just going crazy. It wouldn't have been the first time. He had that kind of effect on her.

Clay stood outside her door. It wasn't his first trip to this destination tonight. He'd walked from his room to hers twice already. But each time, he'd hung back and eventually returned to his own room.

He was asking for trouble.

If he opened the door to her room, if she allowed him to come in, he knew what would happen. Knew there could only be one outcome—if not opening up Pandora's box, at least letting the genie out of the bottle. Everyone knew once that happened, the genie couldn't be stuffed back in.

Better to leave the cork inside, he told himself. She'd obviously moved on with her life, had a child, made a career for herself. If he tried to find his way back into that life, he might mess things up royally, and for no greater reason than his own male pride. She had nothing to gain from the invasion, because he still had his demons, still was no more inclined to settle down now than he'd been before, despite the longing he felt inside. He wasn't husband material, not when the idea of marriage made him want to book the next flight out of town.

About to retreat, Clay heard his pager go off. He looked down at it and saw Santini's number. Whatever crime had gone down on the other end would keep him from making a mistake in his own house.

Grateful for the diversion, he went toward the nearest phone.

He didn't hear Ilene opening the door to her room and stepping out.

She looked up and down the hall, then shrugged.

There was no one there. Her imagination was getting way too active. She could have sworn she'd heard a pager go off. Which meant someone had stood outside her door. The only logical conclusion for her to draw was that it had been Clay.

Only wishful thinking on her part, she admonished herself as she stepped back into her room and closed the door.

Clay didn't want to come back into her life. If anything, he might just want to see if he *could* get back in if he wanted. Only his ego was at work here. He didn't miss her. He didn't want her. She'd already accepted that once, why was it so hard for her to do the second time around?

She went back to something she at least had a fighting chance to understand. The files that were in her computer.

Chapter 10

"But you can't go in there."

The feeble protest was uttered by the diminutive secretary outside of John Walken's office as Clay and his partner made their way past her into the man's domain.

Clay suspected his cousin had already sent in a team of people, armed with a subpoena and boxes to carry off any and all pertinent files that could point to wrongdoings on the part of Walken and other officers of Simplicity Computers.

Walken hung up his phone the moment they entered. Though there was a smile on his lips, the man looked a great deal less hospitable and gregarious than the last time they had seen him. Undoubtedly it had something to do with the possibility of losing his six-million-dollar house, Clay mused. As far as he was concerned, it couldn't have happened to a nicer guy.

Still, Walken went through the motions, rising from behind his desk and making a point of shaking first Santini's hand, then his, as if that silently placed them in a pecking order. Or maybe at odds with one another, Clay wasn't sure. He did know that John Walken had made it to the corporate top by his considerable wits and his talent for reading people.

But he had gotten sloppy, Clay thought. The man had certainly underestimated Ilene.

Walken's smile appeared a little tight as he sat back down. "I'm afraid that if you're here to lead me off in handcuffs, gentlemen, you've gotten ahead of yourselves. The dragoons from the D.A.'s office were just here and carted away a great deal of very dry reading material. It's going to take them a while to falsely piece anything together."

"Thanks for the narrative, Walken," Clay retorted crisply, "but we already know that. We're here on a related matter."

Walken looked to be all graciousness as he leaned back in his chair. "How can I help?"

Clay was going to enjoy wiping that smug look off the man's face when the time came. "We traced two calls from a public phone located about a quarter of a mile away from your house. Both were to the cell phone of a known felon who's not too fussy about what he'd do for money." Clay nailed him with a look. "The same man who left that drawing you claimed not to know anything about taped to Ilene O'Hara's dining room window."

Walken looked bored. "This is all very fascinating, gentlemen, but what does this have to do with me? I'm sure there have been dozens, no hundreds of calls made from that phone. I have a phone in every room of my house, plus two cell phones—one strictly for calls to and from Simplicity—they like keeping me on a short leash here," he confided. "I have absolutely no reason or desire to get into my car and drive down to the gas station to make a call."

Santini pounced. "How did you know it was a gas station? My partner didn't mention where the phone was."

The bored look intensified. "Because there's a gas station a quarter mile from my house and it has a phone, and while I *don't* use the phone, I *do* use the gas pumps." He rose again, his body language clear. He was throwing them out. "Now if you don't mind, I don't think you and I really have anything else to talk about. Despite the 'paper theft' by the D.A.'s office, with Ms. O'Hara no longer working for us, my own workload has increased and I do have reports that need to be done. Can't keep the shareholders waiting forever."

Walken was one cool customer, Clay thought. He hadn't expected any information out of Walken, but he'd just wanted to let him know that the noose was tightening around him. "Out of curiosity, what are you planning on telling those shareholders?"

"That there wasn't as much profit as we first believed there to be." He looked at Clay pointedly. "By the way, if you happen to be in touch with Ms. O'Hara, you might suggest to her that she start looking around for a lawyer of her own."

The goading tone scraped along Clay's already raw nerves. "Are you planning on suing her?"

"No, but the D.A. might want a crack at her," Walken answered mildly. "I'm finding some very curious changes of my own, done not that long ago. All initiated by Ms. O'Hara." The smug look seemed to widen. "I don't have to tell someone as sharp as you that the best way to take attention away from yourself is to create a major diversion. In this case, that would be pointing a finger at the top of the corporate ladder because people always seem so ready to believe the worst of CEOs."

Clay could feel his cheek muscle twitching. The man had a hell of a lot of nerve, trying to turn the tables like this. "And just why do you think that is?"

Walken's face was a mask of innocence. "Haven't the foggiest. But I would alert your so-called witness that I've put all of my best people on this and they are finding some very damning things about her audit." He moved closer to Clay, cutting Santini out for the moment. "Off the record, you might like to suggest to her that she come in so that we can attempt to square things away without any public fanfare.''

Clay knew what the man was after. ''I have no idea where she is.''

Walken looked genuinely disappointed. ''A pity.'' He sighed with just the right amount of regret. ''Then I'm afraid I'm going to have to go on record with the D.A.'s office.''

Clay's expression never wavered. ''I guess you'll just have to.'' About to leave, he paused one last moment as he turned around in the doorway. ''And by the way, 'off the record,' anything happens to her, Walken, anything at all, I'll be back and I won't waste my time chasing after middle men.''

Like a man who'd heard a trap snap successfully, Walken's eyes shifted to Santini. ''You heard him threaten me.''

But Santini merely shook his head. ''Sorry, it's this old water polo injury. Did something to my hearing. It goes in and out at the damnedest times.'' His mouth curved. ''Like now.'' He looked at Clay. ''We finished here, partner?''

''Finished,'' Clay affirmed, leading the way out. ''See you in court, Walken.''

For the rest of the day, Clay felt as if he was just marking time. Beyond looking out for Ilene and her son's safety, the case involving Simplicity was predominantly out of his hands. Other cases awaited him, cases that had been put on hold this past week.

He couldn't do a thing about Walken right now, and it galled him. The man was sharp, not allowing anything to link him to the small-time thug he'd employed to frighten Ilene. Or worse.

Still, everyone slipped up. It was just a matter of being patient, something he didn't have all that much experience with. Clay just liked to keep things moving.

When things got too serious, required too much maintenance, he moved on. Because to remain meant to get too deeply involved. That left you open for a whole world of hurt and he'd already had hurt in his life. He didn't need any more of it.

Shedding his weapon and holster and placing them on the same shelf his father had placed his revolver on for over thirty years, Clay made his way to the back of the house. His mind was on a cold beer and a place where he could just sit down and drain his head of thought for a while. But he walked past the small room that his father had always laughingly referred to as his den. A pool of light spilled from the room out into the hallway.

Clay looked in automatically. Inside the room was a desk, a recliner and a television set, the latter far smaller than the one in the family room.

Inside the room was also Ilene.

She sat at the desk, surrounded by mounds of paper. His father's taxes, he surmised. Clay had a sneaking suspicion that his dad had added things just to keep her busy. Numbers weren't Andrew's passion, but they weren't his nemesis the way he'd indicated, either. His father had always liked to keep on top of things, that included things like his finances and taxes. As long as Clay could remember, his father had never gone to a consultant. It was a matter of pride. Clay knew for a fact that his father had mailed his previous year's return an entire week early. Ilene was surrounded by bunk—previous papers pulled out of sequence and thrown down to give her busywork to do. His father had done it to distract her.

The beer was forgotten. Leaning against the doorjamb, Clay watched as she chewed on her lower lip. She did that when she was lost deep in thought. He'd noticed the habit a long time ago and teased her about it. He'd asked what made her lower lip so tempting to chew on, then had gone on to explore the issue himself by nibbling on it. Her subsequent moan had almost driven him crazy.

Just as memories of her, of them, took their toll on him now.

Ilene was being watched. The feeling had her jerking up her head, first to look toward the window, then at the doorway. A small gasp mingled with a sigh of relief escaped her lips when she realized that it was only Clay watching her.

Next moment the concern returned. Something was up. It was early. Clay didn't come home early, not even for his sister's party. She'd been here for over a week now. The comings and goings of the

Cavanaughs had become second nature to her. Clay left early and returned late, acting far more dedicated than she'd ever thought he would be.

Or maybe having her around prompted him to stay away, she thought. He hadn't kissed her since the night of the party, and acted as if he had to atone for a mistake.

Either that or he'd just been curious to see if there was any of that old spark still left.

She didn't know about his side, but there was spark to spare on hers. It was getting harder and harder for her to ignore.

Setting aside the mountain of papers, she smiled wearily. "How long have you been standing there?"

"Not that long." Straightening, he walked into the room.

"Is this what you do for recreation? Carry on surveillance on the members of your household?"

His grin was slightly lopsided just like his father's, she'd noted. "Nobody in the house was ever as pretty as you to look at."

It was a silly compliment, so there was no reason for her to feel what she was feeling. No reason for her breath to grow short.

"I see you haven't lost your touch." She pushed aside the mountain of papers beside her. "Something's wrong, isn't it?" She turned the swivel chair around to look at him. "Tell me."

He knew he should keep the information to himself. He was a cop, and she was a civilian. Moreover, this did involve her, and he might be alerting her.

But they had history and in his heart, he knew she couldn't be guilty. Knew that if she'd encountered something wrong, she'd blow the whistle on it despite any danger to herself. She had one of those pure souls that knew no compromise.

Still Walken's allegations echoed in his brain.

And people did change.

He sat down on the edge of the desk, looking down at her. "I went to see Walken today."

She had no idea why the air suddenly stood still in her throat. "And?"

"He seems to think he has something on you." He looked at her for a long moment. Realizing that she was still the most beautiful woman he'd ever seen.

"Does he?"

Stunned, Ilene stared at him. Blackmail? It wasn't possible. She lived like a nun outside the office. What could that bastard think he had on her? And why would Clay even have to ask?

"Look, if he's trying for character defamation, he's going to have to go on the Internet and buy someone's life, because mine's so boringly normal and uneventful it would put an insomniac to sleep." An ironic smile twisted her mouth. "That is, up until a couple of weeks ago—"

He stopped her before she could continue. "Walken's not out to destroy you personally, Ilene, he's out to destroy you professionally.''

''Professionally?'' she echoed, confused. ''I don't understand.''

This was harder for him to say than he'd expected. Because he had to play devil's advocate rather than assure her that he didn't believe a word of it, that he knew her integrity was intact. ''He says he found things on your computer that implicate you, that he's willing to talk to you in private.'' His eyes held hers. He owed her that. ''Was there anything?''

Ilene felt as if the lifeboat line had suddenly been yanked from her hand, leaving behind a painful rope burn.

Clay doubted her.

She felt sick to her stomach.

''You have to ask?''

He set his mouth hard. ''I'm a cop. Yes, I have to ask.''

She lifted her chin, damning him to hell. She'd gotten along after he'd left her the first time and she would get along now. All she needed him for was to protect her son's life. Her eyes narrowed.

''Then this is for the cop. No, there's nothing Walken could use against me, unless he planted it himself. But you might want to ask the cop if he has any idea where my friend went. The one who knows I wouldn't ever, ever do anything like that.'' Though she'd tried not to, she was shouting at him.

"I wouldn't have done it even when I needed the money, much less now."

He held his hands up as if to ward off her words and her anger. "Look, don't get mad at me, I'm just trying to do my job."

"I'm not mad, I'm frustrated." Ilene struggled to rein in her emotions. She'd given up making excuses for Walken in her mind. "I didn't do anything wrong, and my son and I have to live like fugitives while the man who hoodwinked God-knows-how-many people goes on living the good life." How could she have been taken in by Walken like that? she upbraided herself. But then, she had a history of doing that. Believing in people destined not to live up her expectations. Like Clay.

"Not for much longer. We'll get the bastard, Ilene," he promised.

Promises didn't help what she was going through now. She looked at him. "We live in the present, not the future. Isn't that something you once said to me?"

He lifted a dismissive shoulder, letting it drop again. "Sounds like something I'd say. I said a lot of stupid things when we were together." He reached for her hand. "One of them was goodbye."

She pulled her hand back, getting up from the chair. "Don't." She wasn't strong enough right now to keep a level head. Not to fall into the same old trap she'd fallen into before.

He got off the desk. She was right. He shouldn't

be coming on to her like that. Trouble was, whenever he was in a room with her, he couldn't think straight.

"Okay, I'll back off. And I had to ask, for the record. In here," he tapped his temple. "I know that you wouldn't cheat, wouldn't lie. Hell, outside of my family, you're the most honest person I know."

Guilt took another pass at her, riddling her with tiny, painful bullets. She couldn't have him thinking she was a plaster saint, not when there was this living, breathing secret between them. "Clay—"

"Yes?"

The words froze in her throat. She was afraid that if she told him the truth now, everything that had come before would disintegrate. She'd be nothing more than a liar to him and he would never be able to believe her again. So she rallied and focused on the larger dilemma.

"Would it be breaking any rules if we went to my house? Tonight?"

"Why—?"

"If John Walken intimated that I was guilty of something, then maybe he planted something either at work or at home."

Other possibilities had occurred to her. Walken might have had her computer doctored at work, or set up a false bank account in her name. He had access to her social security number. How difficult could it be?

Ilene knew she could look for the information on

the Internet tonight, but going to her house was a good place to start.

"No, it wouldn't be breaking any rules," he told her. Bending them a little, maybe, but not breaking. He crossed back to the doorway again. "I'll tell Teri to keep an eye on Alex for us."

It amazed her how easily his family had taken to her son and vice versa. She couldn't help wondering what everyone would say if they knew that they were spending time with that first grandchild Andrew had mentioned at Rayne's birthday party.

At least Rayne would be happy to be off the hook, she thought philosophically.

"Oh my God."

Ilene enunciated each word in a horrified whisper as she looked around the foyer and the living room that lay just beyond. It looked as if a tornado had gone through it, leaving nothing untouched, nothing standing in its original place.

Even the sofa, denuded of cushions, was moved several feet over, standing perpendicular to the wall.

Her breath backing up in her lungs, Ilene was afraid to go any further. Behind her, she heard Clay's voice. He was already on his cell phone, calling in this latest invasion into her life.

She felt numb, felt like crying, but she couldn't allow it to. The state of the house represented the state of her life right now, she thought. Everything had been tossed out on its ear.

Not all that unlike the way it had been when she and Clay had broken up and she'd opted to keep her baby. She'd been alone then, refusing to ask for help from her parents, and instead relying on the money she'd managed to save. She'd stretched it so far it almost tore. It had been the bleakest period of her life.

And without her realizing it, the tears came, silently sliding down her cheeks as she stared at the damage. She didn't know how to begin to set her life in order again.

Clay closed his cell phone and turned toward her. The tears threw him for a moment. He hated seeing a woman cry. Hated seeing Ilene cry even more. If Walken had been in front of him right now, he would have had trouble keeping his hands off the man's neck.

"Don't worry, I'll have the family come over. We can get this place back in shape in no time, right after forensics goes through it."

She shook her head, refusing the offer. "And what about my life?" she cried. "How are we going to get that back in order? How about Alex's life? He's just a little boy and he's a fugitive."

"It's all in the spin, Ilene, and he's got a good one." Clay would have been hard-pressed to have come up with a kid that was happier or better adjusted than Alex. "He's a little boy on an outing with his mother, staying with friends."

At a loss as to what to do, Clay took her into his arms.

At first she fought him, fought against the feeling of wanting to collapse there and just cling to him, cling to something that was stable and wouldn't fall apart. But she was desperate. Surrendering, she let her hands slide down from his chest and just allowed the sobs to come. They racked her body.

He held her for a long time, stroking her hair, whispering something about it being all right. She didn't make out the words, only the sound.

And it helped.

Finally, feeling like a supreme idiot, Ilene raised her head away from his chest and looked up at him. "I'm getting your shirt all wet."

He grinned, his heart aching for her. "It's wash-and-wear, don't worry about it. We're going to have to look around," he told her, "to see if they took anything." That it might have been a robbery was something that never crossed his mind. The television set was still there, as were the stereo components. But something might be missing because whoever was the intruder had been looking for something beyond just revenge.

Ilene shook her head. "I have a feeling they were looking for my laptop."

The computer was safe at his father's house. So were she and her son, theoretically. Only someone out of their right mind would try to break into a place that housed four law enforcement agents.

But right now she was still very much exposed, very vulnerable. And he had no way of helping her with that beyond what he was doing.

Clay looked down at her tear-stained face and began wiping away the telltale tracks with his thumb. And then he did the only thing he could. The only thing he'd wanted to do since the party.

He brought his mouth down on hers and kissed her, hoping something there would reassure her and make her realize that before he'd allow anything to happen to her, he'd give up his life.

He'd give up his life for her, but he wouldn't give his life to her.

The irony of it vaguely struck Clay as he lost himself in a kiss he'd meant to offer only as comfort.

Chapter 11

He wanted her.

There was no use denying it. He wanted Ilene with a fierce, fiery passion that threatened to consume him if he didn't find a way to contain it.

But just for this moment, for this small, fragile instant in time, he let himself go.

Let the kiss deepen. Let her know without words, in the only way he knew how, that she wasn't alone in what she was facing. That he was there for her to lean on, to turn to. She didn't even have to ask.

If desires and passions rose up to try to ensnare him, the way they never could with any other woman, well, that was his problem to deal with. And somehow, he would. Later.

She let herself go. Let go of the reins she'd been clinging to so tightly. It felt wonderful.

And she realized she loved him.

Had always loved him, even when he was no longer part of her life. Because he still was, really. Every time she looked into her son's deep-blue eyes, gazed into his remarkable face, she saw Clay. Saw him in the way his mouth curved when he laughed, saw him in the way Alex drew his eyebrows together when he was being stubborn. There was no use pretending otherwise. Clay was part of her life, every waking, breathing moment of it.

And he was here now, kissing her and blotting out all reason.

His arms tightened around her, insulating her from the outside world with all its cruelty, its danger. Even though she knew it wasn't logical, Ilene felt safe. Secure.

The sound coming in from outside the small circle that Clay had created around her was soft at first, then more insistent when it returned. By the third time, it sounded as if Santini was in serious need of a lung transplant.

Embarrassed, Ilene sprang away from Clay as if he'd suddenly turned into a hot pot handle she was grasping. She could feel warmth flushing her cheeks, and she deliberately avoided looking at Clay.

Santini gave no indication he'd walked in on anything more personal than a detective calming a victim. Instead, he looked around the room, his eyes sweeping over the chaos that had once been the bits and pieces of her everyday life. "The rest of the house look like this?"

Feeling self-conscious and struggling not to, Ilene was grateful for the diversion. "I haven't checked yet, but it looks like they went through everything."

Santini paused for a split second to look at his partner before shaking his head. "Can you tell if they took anything?"

Ilene looked around again. Whoever had been here had deliberately broken almost everything they had touched. Was it because they were angry at not finding the laptop, or were they just sending her another message? Her insides trembled with anger, with an awful feeling of impotent rage.

The small handprint Alex had made for her last Mother's Day caught her eye. The bright blue plaster was shattered in three pieces, its paint chipped around the jagged edges. Ilene stooped and picked the pieces up. Very gently, she placed them on the coffee table, struggling not to cry again. Struggling to pull pieces of herself together.

"Not that I can see," she answered numbly.

Santini nodded. "Not a burglary." He turned to Clay. "Another scare tactic?"

Clay fought the urge to put his arms around her again. He knew she wouldn't appreciate it, especially not with someone else in the room. He reminded himself that she was a hell of a strong woman, but she looked so damn frail right now. "That, or they were looking for her laptop."

"Which you have," Santini assumed, looking at Ilene for confirmation.

She turned from the broken mold. "Which I have."

"Good," he said. Scratching his head, he looked around. Clay knew what his partner was thinking. To the civilian, untrained eye, this still looked like a burglary. Which was right up their alley. Santini turned to him, a hint of an ironic smile on his lips. "Looks like we're back in the game."

"Looks like," Clay agreed. Taking out his handkerchief, he opened it and placed it on the desk beside the broken handprint. He moved the pieces into it and then folded the cloth around it. "I can fix this," he promised Ilene.

"Forensics is on its way," Santini told him. "Why don't you take the lady back and I'll stay here and wait for them?"

They could read each other without words, he and Santini. At times this annoyed him. Right now he was grateful for it.

"Thanks." Clay placed his hand comfortingly on her shoulder and led her out the door.

Ilene muttered "Goodbye" as an afterthought as she let herself be led back to Clay's vehicle. She saw a squad car approaching in the distance, saw curtains moving across the street as one of her neighbors, drawn by the noise and sight of unknown cars, looked on.

Feeling numb and shaken by the attack on her

home, not to mention Clay's earth-shattering kiss, she dropped into the passenger seat. Only when Clay reached over to take the seat belt from its resting position and move it around her did she remember to buckle up.

"He didn't say anything," she finally commented as Clay started up his car.

He guided the car onto the road. "Who?"

"Your partner." Then, because she knew she was being obscure, she added, "When he walked in on us, he didn't say anything."

Clay grinned. His partner always knew when and when not to talk. "Santini's a good guy."

A hostile feeling came out of nowhere. "Does he see that a lot?"

Clay squeezed past the light, wanting nothing more than to get her home. She needed to work at putting this all behind her. "What?"

Exasperated, she waved her hand vaguely. Damn it, she'd gotten carried away by him when she should have kept her feet firmly planted on the ground. What was wrong with her?

"You kissing witnesses, or victims, or whatever the hell category I fall into."

The sharp tone alerted him. He glanced in her direction, looking for confirmation, before he snaked his way onto the freeway. "Are you trying to pick a fight with me?"

About to snap "No," she caught herself and took

stock. If she was coming unglued, she wasn't about to do it here, in his car, where he could watch.

"I don't know what I'm trying to do." A shaky sigh escaped her lips as she scrubbed her hand over her face. She was behaving exactly the way she always hated women to behave, like a shrew. "My emotions are all over the board and I can't seem to get hold of them."

"You need to feel normal."

"I'm not sure I'd know what that is anymore." A slight smile curved her lips.

Impulse mingled with instinct, prompting his next suggestion. "How about I show you? Saturday, why don't you and I take Alex out to the amusement park? Let him have a good time." As he eased his foot down on the brake, Clay looked at her. "Let you watch him have a good time."

Gratitude flooded through her. "How is it that you always seem to know the right medicine for me?"

"Instinct." His eyes were back on the road. The freeway on-ramp was just ahead. "I never lost it when it came to you."

Except for once, she thought, but she kept that to herself. There was no point in ruining the moment for either of them.

The following Saturday, stirred up by the promise of an outing, Alex bounced out his bed and into her room at the ungodly hour of five in the morning.

Ready to roll, he was the very picture of unharnessed excitement.

It had taken her hours to fall asleep and she'd only been at it for less than four. Ilene attempted to rouse herself, even tried to feed off Alex's energy. But it wasn't quite enough to successfully transport her from the land of the comatose.

She caught his hand as he bounced up and down again. "The park doesn't open until nine, honey."

His enthusiasm didn't dim by one iota. "We can wait by the door." His eyes sparkled with glee. "We can be first in line."

That's what happens when a mother teaches her child to be early, she thought as she suppressed a moan.

"Why don't we compromise and wait until eight to leave?" The park was only twenty minutes away by traffic jam. Closer if the cars were moving. It wouldn't take very long to get there and she doubted Clay would appreciate having to hurry up only to stand in line on his day off. His willingness to take them out was enough. With their present set of circumstances, she and her son couldn't risk being out in public without Clay's protection.

Alex gave a mighty sigh, obviously not thrilled at the compromise. Grinning, Ilene threw back the covers and patted the space next to her. Happiness was restored as he wiggled in beside her.

He curled up at her side like a kitten. "I like it

here, Mama," he announced unnecessarily. "Everybody's nice to me."

She never lost an opportunity to drive the point home. "That's because you're such a polite boy."

Alex snuggled into the crook formed by her arm. "Mr. Andrew plays with me a lot. He plays really good." The grin almost split his face as he looked up at her. "He's fun."

The correction was automatic. "He plays really *well.*"

Curiosity took the small brows and sculpted them into a pyramid. "Does he play with you, too?"

Unable to bite it back any longer, Ilene laughed and hugged him to her just before she began to tickle him. The sound of his laughter gladdened her soul.

The sound wove its way through the opened vents of the house, working into the fabric of sleep that surrounded the other household members.

Lying awake in his bed, his hands clasped under his head, Clay heard Alex laughing and smiled to himself without realizing it.

"I think you managed the impossible." Holding the front door open for him, Ilene whispered the words to Clay. The hour was late, and she should have felt like drooping, but she was far too energized, far too wired to realize just how tired she was.

Clay was carrying her son, their son, she amended

silently, in his arms, and the sight had almost made her cry. They looked so right together.

For a split second, the words actually hovered on her lips. *Clay, I've got something to tell you. Alex is your son.* But even now, in the midst of this warm, happy feeling, she felt an iron bar of fear. The words faded without ever being uttered.

Walking into the house, Clay glanced over his shoulder. "How's that?"

She nodded at Alex. Heading toward the stairs in the darkened house, she let Clay go first. "I didn't think it was possible, but you've exhausted him."

As he made his way to Alex's room, Clay laughed under his breath. "The feeling is mutual. He pretty much exhausted me."

Clay deposited the boy on the bed his brother used to sleep in. Quickly he took off Alex's shoes, then moved to cover him with the edge of the blanket. Ilene started to unbutton the boy's shirt, but he stayed her hand.

"Why don't you leave him in his clothes? That way you won't risk waking him up." Then, in case she needed further convincing, he added, "I used to fall asleep in my clothes all the time."

Ilene withdrew and let him cover Alex. Glancing over toward the window, she saw that the gathering clouds had finally decided to empty. It was drizzling very lightly. "Looks like we made it home just in time."

For a moment she stared out the window. The rain reminded her of the first time he'd kissed her.

Stop, don't spoil a wonderful day, don't let yourself go.

Mounting a mental defensive against the onslaught of memories, Ilene switched on the nightlight Andrew had given her for Alex. He'd told her that it had once belonged to Clay, who'd used it for more than half a dozen years to chase away any demons that might have been lurking in the shadows. The story had made her smile.

Her heart swelled as she brushed back the hair from her son's face. Ilene slipped out of the room. Clay was right behind her and he eased the door shut.

She didn't want the day to end, but it edged its way to midnight. "Thank you for today," she murmured, lingering by the door. "He had a really wonderful time."

Clay leaned his hand on the wall just above her head, creating intimacy out of a space in the hall. "Yeah, I know." The boy had thanked him more than once, and he'd been on the receiving end of several heartfelt hugs. It surprised Clay to realize just how much he liked them. "He doesn't exactly keep things bottled up inside. How about you?"

He was so close now, all she had to do was rise up on her toes and brush her lips against his. And invite trouble. But trouble had taken on a very pleasing form. "How about me what?"

His eyes never left hers as they stirred up everything inside. He began to play with the end of her hair. "Did you have a good time?"

Breathing became more difficult for her. "Mothers always have a good time when their kids enjoy themselves." Copping out, she looked away.

He cupped her cheek and brought her around until her eyes met his again. "I'm not talking to Alex's mother, I'm talking to you. To Ilene O'Hara." His voice lowered so that it didn't carry beyond the small perimeter their bodies formed. "Did you have a good time today?"

She smiled then, one of those smiles that really got to him, curling up in his stomach and then spreading out all through him. Leaving him wanting more. Wanting her. "Yes, I had a good time."

"How good?"

The words teased along her face, making her tighten like a bow that ached for release. Her throat felt dry as she said, "Very, very good."

His eyes smiled into hers. "Yeah, me, too."

She desperately sought something to say, not to just stand here like some pie-faced, moony idiot, dissolving in a puddle right before his eyes. "He likes you, you know. Alex. He likes everyone here."

"That's good," he murmured softly. "Because we all like him." Weaving his fingers through her hair, he slowly slid them along her scalp. Making her tingle. Awakening anticipation.

She could feel her pulse speeding up, her heart

beginning to go into its dance, the one it did every time he was so close to her. Every time she wanted him. This time was no different.

"By the way, did I thank you for gluing his hand-print together?"

"Yes—" his eyes held her "—you did."

Afraid of what she was feeling, she struggled to draw away, but only managed to place less than a fraction of an inch between them. "Clay, this is getting complicated."

"No," he said so softly the word all but floated along her skin like magical fairy dust, "it's getting simple. Very, very simple."

"No pun intended," she breathed, mesmerized by the look in his eyes.

"None," he assured her. His fingers curved along her throat, he tilted her head back.

And then he kissed her.

Again.

Just like the first time.

That same wild crash of thunder echoed in her head as he drew her up to him, holding her closely, his hands on her shoulders. That same delicious, intoxicated feeling spilled through her veins even as her adrenaline poured in from every source.

Her head was spinning and she made no effort to make it stop, made no effort to end the wild ride before it became too dizzying for her. With her whole body and soul, she wanted this, wanted to have him make love to her, with her, just one last time.

Maybe she was crazy; she didn't know. But after all she'd been through these past couple of weeks, she felt she deserved a little crazy. And a little happy as well. No matter what else was involved, she did know this: Clay made her happy, if only for the moment.

She wrapped her arms around his neck, cleaving her body to his, igniting the fuse that was so short it was almost nonexistent.

Over and over again his mouth shifted over hers, kissing her from all angles, getting lost in the taste and feel of her.

But even as he assaulted her lips, he felt her smile against his mouth. He drew his head back to look at her uncertainly. "What?"

"You taste of cotton candy." To underscore her point, she ran her tongue along her lips.

Clay could feel desire taking large chunks out of his restraint. "And you taste of everything I've ever wanted."

She fell off the edge.

If there'd been any sort of hope left for her retreat, any chance of backtracking, it was gone now. Evaporated. The last of her resolve had melted in the heat of his mouth, in the heat of his eyes.

But mostly it had disappeared because of what he'd said.

Sealing her mouth to his, she kissed him hard and

with every fiber of her being. And in one smooth movement, the captured became the captor. Her lips never leaving his, Ilene reached behind her and found the doorknob. She turned it and managed to open the door to her room.

The action registering on his fevered brain, Clay stopped for a moment and looked at her. Because it was Ilene, because he felt the things he was feeling, things he wasn't about to put a name to, he held himself in check. One more moment and there would be no turning back. "Are you sure?"

She laughed softly as she looked up at him. "This is no time to interrogate the witness, Detective."

"No," he agreed. "Maybe not."

The next moment he brought his mouth back down on hers and scooped her up in his arms.

Shouldering the door so that it opened wider, he carried her into her room, then eased it closed again with his back. He didn't want the sound carrying, didn't want to risk having anyone come out of their rooms to look for her, or ask questions about the outing. That was for tomorrow.

Tonight, at long last, was for lovemaking.

He placed her on the bed, wanting nothing more than to join her, than to be joined with her, but he still felt she needed a moment to think, to be sure, even though she'd said she was.

Even though he knew that if she changed her mind, he would most likely implode sometime during the course of the night.

Moving away from the bed, he went first to the adjoining bathroom and flipped the lock on the door, then to the door that led out into the hallway and repeated the action.

Amused, she raised herself up on her elbow. ''Locking me in?''

''Just making sure Alex's education doesn't take a quantum leap tonight.''

He was being thoughtful. Damn the man, how was she supposed to ever work him out of her system when he continued to do things like this? He cared about her son, and being nice to Alex was the fastest way into her heart.

''Why?'' she murmured teasingly to hide the very real case of nerves she was developing. Her eyes never left him as he crossed back to her bed. ''Just what would he be learning?''

''That the birds and bees have got nothing on us.'' Lying down beside her, Clay continued talking as he started to unbutton the front of her blouse. ''That there are some things about being an adult that make the whole experience worthwhile, even though a lot of it's just a huge pain in the—butt,'' he said at the last moment.

She could feel her skin quivering as the buttons came out of their holes and the material parted, exposing her to him.

His hand slowly glided along her belly, creating havoc, bringing a strange sort of unsettling peace at the same time.

None of it made any sense to her. The only thing that mattered was that she was here with him and that they were going to make love.

Unable to remain passive any longer, she sat up and dragged his shirt from his torso. Tossing it on the floor, she covered his bare chest with her own, fusing her mouth to his.

The heat that erupted nearly singed them both.

It didn't matter. She was where she belonged, where she'd always belonged. With everything she had ever endured, the only place that was home to her, that had ever *been* home to her was here, in his arms.

She meant to make the most of it.

Chapter 12

There was no containing his eagerness and no reason to. Whatever else had gone down between them, they had never played coy with each other, never pretended to be indifferent to each other. The attraction had sizzled between them from the very first.

Clay wanted to go slowly, even though everything inside of him raged for release, for that final, exhilarating moment when he was joined with her and the pinnacle was reached. But he also wanted to savor the moment, the journey.

Her.

So he undressed Ilene more slowly than the passions slamming against him demanded. He undid the button at her jeans, then slipped his hand inside, his fingers tantalizingly strumming along her belly as they dipped lower and lower until they finally reached the warmth, taking possession of her.

Ilene twisted and moaned against him, driving him insane with excitement, with desire.

The heat of her loins urged him onward, the heat of her mouth as she kissed his lips and face over and over sealed his fate.

Unable to stand the confines of her clothing any longer, Ilene took matters into her own hands. She wiggled out of her jeans, still moving against him, obviously driving him wild. She felt him grow hard wanting her. The feeling of power sent her head reeling.

"Damn, but I've missed you," Clay muttered between gasps of breath that continued to grow shorter and shorter.

"Less talk, more action."

It was an order, followed by a laugh as she scrambled to yank his jeans and briefs from his body, moving both aside with one determined swift jerk of her wrists. Before he could make a move, like a person driven she raced kisses along his torso, branding him, enflaming him even more than he thought was humanly possible.

But then, she'd always had that effect on him. Entirely unpredictable, making him forget everything but her while she was in his arms.

It was only after, when the twilight crept into his soul, that he remembered. Remembered that nothing was forever, that everything could be gone in a heartbeat, leaving behind only insurmountable pain. He'd seen it in his father's eyes, seen it in his own reflection in the mirror after his mother vanished. Ultimately, that was what had driven him away from Ilene, the fear of loss. He told himself that if he never allowed himself to become too attached, then separation would never be a problem. He'd told himself that lie so often over the years, he'd begun to believe it.

But Ilene was back now, at least for the moment, and he meant to enjoy this to the fullest, enjoy her to the fullest. Before she was gone again.

It was hard to pace himself, reining himself in when she captured his senses and his body. Twice he'd felt himself tottering dangerously on the brink, especially when her cool fingers had cupped him possessively.

With monumental effort, Clay shifted positions until he was on top of her. Grasping her hands above her head and holding them in place with one of his own, he turned the tables on her.

The claiming began slowly. A kiss to each shoulder, to the outline of her collarbone, to the space between her breasts before he feasted on each one.

And all the while he worked his way ever inward and downward.

By the time he'd reached the hollow of her belly, she felt as if she was literally on fire and desperate to have him put it out.

Ilene wrapped her legs around his upper torso, arching her body against him. Craving release, craving the delicious sensations she hadn't felt for so long. Because once he'd left her life, there had been no one else. She couldn't let there be. Clay Cavanaugh had been the one love of her life, the one major disappointment. After he'd gone, she'd vowed never to be so exposed again.

But yet, here she was, exposed in more ways than just one. And she didn't care. Not now. All she wanted was what only he could give her.

She felt his tongue caressing her, stroking the velvet softness. Biting down on her lip, she silenced the whimper that welled up within her throat as she felt the sensation building to a crescendo.

The first explosion racked her body even as the beginnings of the next one followed in its wake.

His mouth created wonderful upheavals within her body, exhausting her, priming her. Making her ready for him.

Ilene tried to follow suit, to make him as insane with desire as he'd made her, but she doubted he could feel the levels, the layers that she was experiencing.

It didn't matter.

For this one moment in time, he wanted her; she could see it in his eyes. He wanted her more than anything and it was enough.

When she thought that there wasn't an inch of her body that wasn't completely exhausted, he came to her, and pulled himself into position. Looming above her, his eyes held hers as he drove himself inside of her. Ilene was so far enveloped with desire, she saw nothing else, felt nothing else, only him, only this feeling.

A bittersweetness hovered just beyond. Because it would be over, and when it was, the sadness would come. But not yet, not yet.

And when the final moment came, when their bodies rocked simultaneously, she tightened her arms around him, whispering his name against his ear. Whispering she loved him within her soul.

Slowly the passion subsided and the euphoria mellowed into a soothing murmur rather than a roar. He gathered her to him and kissed the top of her head. After the passion came a deep-rooted affection.

"You've gotten more agile." He pretended to peer at her face. "Should I be jealous?"

What she did she did by instinct, because she was with him and he brought it out in her. "You never had anything to be jealous about." She turned her face toward him, her cheek resting against his arm. "You were always in a class by yourself."

"What about Alex's father?" He'd promised himself not to ask, but he couldn't help it. If Alex wasn't his, then someone else had come after him. Someone else had made love with her, maybe even made her fall in love with him. Was that man as totally out of the picture as she'd said? "Was he in a class by himself?"

Yes, because he's you.

"You might say that." She rose up on her elbow to look at Clay. She didn't want to be pulled into a discussion where she might trip up. "Look, I don't want to talk about Alex's father, or about any of the legions of women who came after me."

"No legions," he assured her. "Just pale, puny shadows, Ilene." Slipping his hand beneath her head, he tilted it up so that their eyes held. He wanted her to believe him. "Nobody has ever meant anything to me but you."

Ilene pulled her head back, away from his touch. "Don't say things like that." Hearing him made her want to believe him, and they both knew that was a mistake. "We both know this isn't going to go anywhere."

She was right, he thought.

Or was she?

Something within him protested, that she was making assumptions that might not be true. But he knew himself, knew that as much as he wanted her, being with Ilene ultimately scared him.

So he reverted to humor and used it to camouflage his feelings.

"Let's see, the subject of your love life and mine are both closed and you don't want me to tell you how you were always the only one. That doesn't leave us very much to discuss." He turned toward her, threading a strand of her hair through his fingers. He sniffed it without thinking, breathing in the herbal scent. "So what do we do with the rest of the night?"

She knew that look, delighted in that look and could feel herself reacting to it immediately. "I think we both know what we really want to do with the rest of the night."

Her grin was broad, inviting. She was already shifting, bringing her torso even closer to his. He felt his body respond in direct proportion. "You always could read my mind."

"Not your mind." The excitement took hold as he pressed a kiss to the hollow of her throat. She wiggled a little, drawing his heat to her. "But other signs I got pretty good at reading."

He smiled into her eyes before he kissed her again and wrapped the world around the two of them.

She couldn't remember when she'd been happier with Clay. Even taking into account the time she'd spent with Clay when they were both far younger than now, she hadn't been as happy as this.

For the first time in his life, her son was entrenched in the bosom of a real family, not the two separate factions that made up her parents and their spouses. Alex was thriving. She only had to look into his eyes to see it.

As for herself, there were no words to describe how she felt. Yes, professionally she was still standing on the edge of a huge abyss, but privately, it was another matter. She and Clay stole moments in the middle of the night, when he would come to her or she to him and then they would find their way to paradise together.

The days melted into one another, and another week passed. She knew that each day was a gift, but at the same time, each day only brought her closer to the end, to a time when all this would be over and she would have to return to her own life.

For now she was determined to savor this situation brought on by the worst of circumstances. It only went to show you, as she'd always tried to maintain, there wasn't anything bad that happened that some good didn't come out of it.

Right now that good was being with Clay again.

If her nights were filled with Clay, her days were kept busy in a different way. She worked on Andrew's taxes, squaring away both the year that had come before as well as putting his current affairs in order.

"Don't know what to say," Andrew murmured, looking over the neatly printed pages she'd presented him with.

"You don't have to. The look on your face says it all."

"Damn, if you were twenty years older, or I was thirty years younger, I'd ask you to marry me."

She'd smiled then, amused as well as touched.

"I'm afraid you'd be too much man for me, Andrew."

The look in his eyes told her that he knew more than either one of them was about to say. "In my day I might have been, but I leave that to the younger generation now, like Clay."

He said no more, but things were understood.

Two of those days Ilene also went into the D.A.'s office. One to work with Janelle, who prepped her for her deposition, the other to actually give her deposition. Despite the fact that she had both truth and Janelle on her side, Ilene couldn't help feeling nervous. Simplicity Computers' legal counsel was the best money could buy. No less than six men and women from a top firm descended upon the proceedings, all of a single mind and purpose: to cast aspersions on her credibility.

While she gave her testimony, it felt as if the afternoon would never end. Eventually it did, but not before four and a half hours had gone by. Her mouth was dry despite all the water she'd consumed, and her body was utterly drained.

Twilight had begun to skirt around the half-emptied parking lot by the time she went to her car. She felt like a woman walking in her sleep. Until she saw him. Someone was standing by her car, indolently leaning against it.

Her heart climbed up in her throat, and she looked around to see if there was anyone else around, but there wasn't. She hadn't told anyone about the calls on her cell phone, the ones that uttered a few words of warning in her ear before disconnecting. She hadn't wanted to worry anyone.

Was whoever was making those calls here now?

For a second she thought about hurrying back into the building. There was still a guard on the first floor. Maybe…

She looked again. The stance was familiar. And then she smiled with relief.

Clay.

She stepped up her gait, cutting the distance between them. "What are you doing here?"

He brushed his lips against hers before answering. "I came to give you moral support."

She felt like sighing and leaning against him but didn't want to seem like a clinging vine. Just knowing he was around made her feel stronger.

"You're a little late for that, the deposition is over."

"I know. I figured there was an outside chance you were in shreds right about now and might need a shoulder to lean on." He'd been worried about her, but he knew how determined she was to stand on her own two feet. They both valued their independence. Sometimes too much so. "Don't forget, I've been through the process myself a couple of times. Nothing lawyers like better than sinking their teeth into you for sport." He could have saved himself the concern. "I hear you held your own."

She'd only just now walked out of the conference

room. Some of the unholy six were still upstairs, sitting around the table of torture. "How?"

Clay winked at her. "Oh, I've got my ways." Then, because she looked as if she was ready to take a swing at him, he came clean. Draping his arm over her shoulders, he brought his mouth close to her ear and said, "Janelle came out before you. She said you got through it with flying colors, even though they tried to make you retract your allegations."

Ilene was proud of herself for not folding, but it definitely hadn't been easy. "So you've got spies everywhere I take it."

He laughed and paused to kiss her. "Just about. Hey, it pays to be a Cavanaugh." He kissed her again, then knew he was in danger of not being able to stop once he got started. Nothing seemed like enough with her. One taste led to another, one craving satisfied only gave way to a bigger one. He was already aching for her and nighttime still felt an insurmountably long ways away. "C'mon, I'll take you home."

She looked at the car he'd been leaning against. "What about my car?"

He'd meant in her car. Clay gestured toward it. "I'll drive, you crash—no pun intended."

Ilene took out her keys and handed them to him. "What about your car?" Now that she looked around, she realized she didn't see it.

"At home." He unlocked the passenger side, then

opened the door. "I had Teri drop me off before she went on her big date."

The choice of words intrigued her. She found herself wanting to know things about his family, about their daily lives. Wanting to be part of those daily lives. "Big date?"

But he shook his head. That was for another time. "Long story." He saw the curiosity in her eyes. "I wasn't really listening to her as she told me. I was thinking about you."

Well, she couldn't exactly fault him for that now, could she? He was being sweet.

She got into the car, automatically reaching for the seat belt as he closed the car door for her. Damn, but she was going to hurt when it was over. But she knew better than to assume what was going on between them would turn into something more this time around. Clay was Clay and she couldn't ask him to change. The only thing she could do was hope that he would because he wanted to.

Stop it, she upbraided herself. *He came to pick you up. Be happy with what you have, stop pining after what you want.*

As Clay got in on the driver's side, her cell phone began to ring. The soft noise jarred her, and she instantly stiffened.

When she made no move to reach for her phone, he looked at her. "Aren't you going to answer that?" There was an odd expression on her face. He wondered if something had gone wrong that Janelle hadn't disclosed. Why else would she look like that?

"Sure."

Praying the ringing would cease, she reached into her purse for the phone.

The ringing continued.

Maybe it was a call she wanted, she told herself. Maybe it was even Alex on the other end. Initially feeling that her son needed some stability, she'd written down her number for him. That way he could call her any time he wanted to hear the reassuring sound of her voice.

But even as she flipped open her phone, her gut told her that it wasn't Alex, wasn't anyone she wanted to hear from.

And she was right.

"Don't get too cocky," the metallic voice on the other end of the line warned in response to her tense greeting. "Your time is coming. And once it does, you'll be sorry."

Not bothering to acknowledge that she'd heard a word, Ilene slapped the phone closed.

Clay hadn't started the car. The tense expression on her face had his entire attention. He'd been watching her until she'd abruptly shut the phone without saying a word. "What's the matter?"

Ilene shook her head, firing the word "Nothing" at him.

Definitely not nothing. Clay shifted so that he was directly facing her. His voice was stern now. He spoke to her the way he did to a reluctant witness. "Who was on the phone, Ilene?" They weren't going anywhere until he found out.

She pressed her lips together before launching into a lie. "Nobody. Just someone trying to get me to subscribe to the local paper." She jerked her shoulder into a careless shrug. "I get that sometimes. You'd think that they wouldn't have access to cell phone numbers, but—"

"That wasn't someone trying to get you to subscribe to the local paper. Nuisance calls don't make you turn as pale as a ghost. You're almost translucent, Ilene. Now who was on the phone?"

She shook her head, giving up the pretense. "I don't know. It sounded like E.T."

A voice synthesizer, he thought. He immediately thought of Walken. "All right, what did they say?"

"That my time is coming." She tried to shrug it off again. "Maybe I'm making something out of nothing. Maybe it's just some religious sect—"

"Stop it, Ilene," he ordered. Then, when she fell into silence, he gently took her hands in his. His voice softened. "We both know who it was, or at least, who's behind it." Clay searched her face for some kind of a sign. "This wasn't the first time, was it?"

She took a deep breath, then exhaled before answering. "No."

Clay bit off an oath. Losing his temper with her wasn't going to help. "Why didn't you tell me?"

"What good would it do?" Detective or not, she didn't want him getting hurt on her account. So far, there'd just been veiled threats, a stupid drawing and her house had been trashed, but no one had been hurt. She didn't want Clay to be the first. "He's too smart to make the calls from his house or office. John Walken is a very sharp man. I only caught him because I accidentally came across supply lists and expenses that weren't accounted for. Lists I'm the only one with copies of, because the originals were undoubtedly shredded the second he knew he couldn't buy me off."

He didn't care about lists or inflated stock options. He only cared about what happened to her and Alex. "He can't get away with threatening you."

"And he won't," she insisted. "As long as you keep Alex and me safe. That's the bottom line, Clay, keeping us safe." And then she gave voice to something she'd been wrestling with in the wee hours of the morning, when problems always seemed to be at their worst. "And if you have a choice, if for some reason you can only save one of us, Clay, I want you to swear to me that you'll choose Alex."

About to finally start the car, he stopped again to stare at her. "What the hell are you talking about? It's not an either-or situation."

"But if—"

"You'll be safe, you'll both be safe. Nobody's going to harm either one of you as long as I'm alive. As long as any member of my family is alive," Clay amended. He couldn't cope with her flirting with her own demise. All this past week, he'd fought with his feelings. Always drawn to Ilene, he hadn't thought he could be a good husband, a good father. Both Ilene and her son had been through a great deal and he didn't want to complicate their lives any further.

But try as he might, he couldn't divorce himself from the desire to be with her. He'd developed parental feelings for the boy as well, something he'd never thought possible. He looked forward to coming home after a tough day on the streets, not just to her, but to Alex, to the innocence and purity that he saw in the boy's eyes. Knowing this would end soon was no longer comforting. Now the tranquility of the moment was important, as well.

As was she.

"Don't you get it yet?" Clay added. "My father considers you and Alex family now. There's no way anything is going to happen to you."

She tried to let his words comfort her. And restrained herself from asking him if he felt the same way as his father did about them.

And from telling him right then and there that Alex was his son. Because that path only led to trouble. But it was a path that was becoming increasingly more insistent as it beckoned to her.

Chapter 13

The sigh that escaped her lips seemed to come from deep down in her soul. Clay glanced at her before looking back on the road. "Tired?"

There was a point where she thought the deposition was going to be never ending. Each time one lawyer retired, another barreled in to take his place. She was surprised that her head wasn't throbbing.

The smile she offered him was weary. "I feel as if someone's vivisected me, then put me back together using a blunt needle and fishing tackle."

The light turned red. He gave her more than a fleeting look. "Well, they did an admirable job of it. You look terrific."

Without thinking, she touched his cheek, a fondness filtering through her. He really did know the right thing to say at times. "Thanks, I needed that."

The light turned green. He eased his foot back on the accelerator. "Anything else you need, I'm here for you."

"Are you?" The question came out before she could stop it.

"You know I am." He looked at her again though the traffic was thick.

Ilene wanted to believe that he would be there for her, not just today, but tomorrow and the day after that, straight on to infinity, but she knew differently, had been abruptly shown differently.

The freeway connection was just ahead. There was a minimall adjacent to it. "Want to stop somewhere for a drink?" Clay asked.

Any other time she might have said yes. But after being shark bait all afternoon, she just wanted to go somewhere to feel safe and pull herself together. "No, straight home is fine." She stared at his profile. It looked somehow stronger in the shadows that were dancing around in her car. "I just need to look at my son."

He understood what she meant. The people you loved were a haven. "He's a great kid." His own words echoed back to him and he grinned. "I never thought I'd hear myself say that about someone who comes up to my belt buckle, but he is." Clay got into the carpool lane as it fed onto the freeway ramp. "You did a great job raising him."

It wasn't finished by any means, but the years so far had been good to her. "He's still a work in progress," she reminded him. "They tell me the roughest part is still ahead." She recalled one friend's on-going lament. "Teenage boys aren't supposed to acknowledge their mother's existence."

"Alex won't be like that."

He said it with such confidence. "What makes you so sure?"

He lifted a shoulder, letting it fall in a noncommittal shrug. "Just a feeling. Not all teenagers ignore their mothers, you know. Shaw didn't. I didn't." Until that infamous, fateful day, he would have said that he was closest to his mother. "Although I did give my father some grief before I settled down. But that was after—" His voice trailed away. Even now he really didn't like to talk about it.

Ilene read between the lines. "After your mother died?"

"Yeah." He sighed. The words sounded so damning. Eyes on the lane next to him, he switched over. "He doesn't believe it, you know, my Dad. He doesn't believe she's dead."

She could understand that. Andrew was a man who was stubborn about his convictions. "Maybe for him, she isn't."

Somehow, because he was talking to Ilene, the words came easier than he thought they would. He found he needed to talk, to share what had been sealed inside for so long. "Every so often I catch him going through the files he kept, looking for something he might have missed the thousand other times he went over the information."

Her heart went out to the older man. And to Clay. She could tell by the tone of his voice that he still had trouble accepting his mother's death himself. "He must have loved her very, very much," she said softly. *And so did you.*

"Yeah, he did." He laughed shortly, remembering. "When we were kids, that was the only redeeming quality our father had, in our eyes—that he loved the same person we did."

She thought of the man who had welcomed her and her son into his home without so much as a pause. A sense of loyalty had her defending him. "I'm sure he must have had others."

"If he did, we never knew about them. We hardly ever saw him," Clay explained. "Longest period of time he was around was when he was recuperating from that gunshot wound he took to the shoulder." He and the others had spent most of the time tiptoeing around out of his father's way. "Talk about a wounded bear," he said, grinning.

Her sense of loyalty couldn't remain silent any longer. "Your father seems like a wonderful man, Clay."

"Yeah," he agreed. "But that came after." He glanced over and saw her puzzled look. "It was as if he felt he had to fill her shoes for us. Become both mother and father." He could remember thinking that the roof had collapsed and that the walls were caving in. "It's a *hell* of an adjustment."

"You're lucky he cared enough about you to do it. Some people just withdraw altogether, refuse to have any contact with anyone, especially their children." She gazed at him for a long moment before looking away. "Not all parents know how to love their children."

"You're talking about yours, aren't you?" The shrug she gave him reflected in the side window. She didn't turn to look at him. "You never mention your parents," he realized.

"That's because there's not much to mention." And because talking about them and their lack of affection hurt. She used to think all parents were cold like that until she discovered it wasn't the case. Not all parents were nearly as self-absorbed as hers was.

"I don't even know if they're still living," he realized. He took the off-ramp and made a hard right. They were almost home.

"Still living," she confirmed. "Somewhere." Her father had written in his last communiqué that he was moving almost eleven months ago. She still didn't have a new address for him. "They have their own lives. I get Christmas cards. Sometimes. We're not close." No matter how much she'd tried when she was young, that hadn't happened. And if anything the birth of her son had only driven them further away.

She turned to look at him. "You don't know how lucky you are to have what you have."

He looked at her significantly as he brought the car to a stop at the curb before his house. "I'm beginning to learn."

More than an hour later, Ilene sighed as she dropped down into the easy chair in the family room. Ordinarily, this was considered Andrew's chair, but he had already gone off to bed.

She offered what she could of a smile to Clay, who looked as if he'd been waiting for her to come down again. Getting Alex to bed had taken her longer than she'd thought. "Well, he's all tucked away. Three readings of *The Cat in the Hat*, but he finally dozed off," she said, feeling as if her eyes could close with little encouragement.

"You look like you're about to doze off, too."

"I am." She tried to rouse herself. "I just came down to say good-night." She looked around. The silence had finally penetrated. "Looks like everyone else turned in early."

"Or turned out," he contradicted. "Teri and Rayne are out for the evening. Dad's in his room." He nodded toward the stairs. "He said something about finishing a good book." He knew that his father was really poring over his mother's files, but it was the kind of open secret neither commented on.

"And what about you?" When they'd been together all those years ago, he'd considered going to bed before two in the morning something that only old people and stick-in-the-muds did. "Are you now this sedate, stay-at-home type?"

There was something to be said for staying home. As long as there was someone important to stay there with you. "Seems that way."

She knew better. Detective or not, he still led a pretty wild life. "Teri told me stories."

"Lies." He looked at her, assuming the angelic face of a choirboy.

She bit back a laugh. "Rayne backed her up."

"Bigger lies." He rose to his feet and crossed to where she was sitting. "Besides, I've turned over a new leaf."

She eyed him innocently. "Why would you have to turn over a new leaf if what your sisters told me were lies?"

"Don't complicate things with logic." She couldn't quite read the look in his eyes. "I have something better at home than I could possibly find outside."

Her grin teased him. "Another way to look at it is you have something at home that doesn't require much effort to get."

"Oh, don't give me that," he hooted. "You take a hell of a lot of effort."

She grinned up at him. Since she'd gotten here, she'd been his for the asking. They both knew that. "Since when is crooking your finger considered a hell of a lot of effort?"

He laughed as he took her hand and pulled her to her feet. Pulled her to him. "C'mere you and stop giving me lip."

She cocked her head, her mouth curving. The stress of the day began to drain away. "I thought that was the whole point."

"The whole point of everything," his voice dropped down to a seductive whisper, "is being here with you."

Framing her face, he brought his mouth down to hers before she could say anything in reply. Brought his mouth down to hers and began that whole wonderful, delicious process again. The one in which her entire system became a whirling blender on the verge of spinning wildly out of control.

Her fingertips digging into his shoulders, she pressed her body against his, taking comfort from his presence, sealing herself to the energy that vibrated between them.

And then he stopped.

Still holding her face in his hands, he drew his head back. "If you're too tired—"

Damn, he couldn't withdraw now. She needed him. Needed the magic they formed together. "The day I'm too tired to kiss you, Clay Cavanaugh, is the day you can start throwing dirt on my cold, dead body."

God, but he loved her. How could he have convinced himself, even for a moment, otherwise? How

could he have believed that he could live his life
without her? "You know what I mean."

She opened her eyes wide, feigning ignorance as
she looked up at him. "No, what do you mean?"

In response, he scooped her up in his arms.
"Witch," he pronounced.

Because she was. She was a witch who'd cast a
spell on him. She made him happier than he ever
thought he could possibly be. And made him realize
how very shallow his existence was without her.
Home, family, career, they all meant a great deal to
him, but without her, without the feeling that
coursed through his veins every time he was with
her, everything else seemed diminished somehow.
Ilene was the spotlight by which everything else was
highlighted.

Even the fear that had dogged his life and haunted
his mind for so long had faded into the background.
It was still there but no longer looming over him.

All because of her.

"I can walk," she protested. "Put me down."

He just kept walking toward the stairs. "And let
you get away? Not likely."

She laced her arms around his neck, amused. Ilene
caught her lower lip between her teeth. "This isn't
exactly torture you're offering me."

He resisted the urge to nibble on her lip. "I'm
taking no chances."

Wonders just never ceased. "Since when have
you become this steadfast person?"

"Since you," he told her. On the landing, he walked into her room and closed the door with his back. "The whole change in me falls directly on your shoulders."

Before she could protest, he deposited her on the bed. She bounced up, scrambling to her knees and moving to the edge of the bed in front of him. There was mischief in her eyes.

Catching hold of his shirt, she pulled him closer to her. "I dare you to say that again," she challenged. "Without your clothes on this time."

He laughed. "Never met a dare I couldn't meet." Spreading his arms wide, he stood before her, ready. Eager. "Do your worst."

"My best," she corrected, her fingers flying down the buttons of his shirt, releasing them. His shirt hung open, and she pushed it back off his shoulders, stripping it from him before she turned her attention to his belt buckle. She only had enough time to unnotch it before he pressed her back against the bed.

"You're getting ahead of me." Joining her, he made quick work of her blouse. The next second, he'd managed to unhook the clasp behind her back. Her bra teasingly moved away from her breasts. He swept it aside with the flat of his hand.

She wiggled against him, her pulse quickening. "I'm the guest, I'm supposed to."

He paused to press a kiss to each breast before answering. "I'm the host, I should lead the way."

Adrenaline filled her veins, hand in hand with desire. "You always have."

He pulled the skirt away from her. Her underwear went the same way. Banter died in his throat as his eyes swept over her.

No matter how many times he saw her like this, he would never tire of it. Never view her passively. Anticipation rose just as it had the first time.

More.

Because he knew what was in store for him.

And because he loved her.

Pulling her down against him, he sealed his body to hers as he kissed her over and over again, losing himself in the process as he made love to every inch of her body. Worshipping her flesh because of the peace and excitement she brought to him each time she surrendered to him. And took him prisoner.

They explored each other's bodies as if the terrain was not firmly etched in their brains, as if they didn't know it far better than their own. The tastes and scents teased and aroused and gave comfort to them in the heat of their passion.

Having brought her to a climax, Clay was about to enter her when she surprised him by suddenly switching positions. Now she was the one on top. She wiggled as she straddled him.

"I thought you were tired," Clay whispered. The heat from her core as it spread over him aroused him more than he thought he could bear.

Her mouth, its outline blurred and mussed from

the imprint of his, widened into a mischievous grin that teased his soul even as it aroused him even further. "Second wind."

He loved the expression in her eyes, loved the way they shone, as if they were sharing some secret joke with him that he had yet to catch on to.

He filled his hands with her hair and dragged her down until his mouth caught hers. The deepening kiss reeled them both in. And then she arched her body and drew him into her, pinning him down with her slight weight.

Clay grasped her hips as she began to move. The pace grew faster and faster until they reached the familiar summit and took it together.

She cried out his name, the sound muffled against his lips.

And when she lay against him, spent, trying to regulate her breathing again, he could only marvel at this creature he'd pushed away once. But not again.

Drawing in air, it took him a second to catch his own breath. "You are full of surprises."

He felt her heart hammering against his chest, felt her hair gliding along his skin as she raised her head to look at him.

"You don't know the half of it," she told him.

Maybe not, he thought, but he was going to spend the rest of his life learning. It was a life sentence he now knew he was more than willing to assume.

* * *

Andrew sat on the family room floor, hunched over a table. Alex sat opposite him, his attention fastened to the artfully arranged dominos between them. The boy's mother had to go back for another meeting with Janelle over more questions that were being raised. The indictment hearing was at the end of the week and they wanted their presentation to be air tight.

He was baby-sitting, not that he minded. There was another reason he wrestled with a dampening sorrow.

The holidays were coming soon. Thanksgiving was just around the corner and then came Christmas. This used to be his favorite time of year. For the sake of his family, he still put on a show, now aided and abetted by an impressive spread. And sometimes it worked. He got caught up in it, and the pain that he lived with, the pain that grew acute this time of year, would hide behind a cloud, waiting. Biding its time until he had a free moment, and then it would creep up behind him and explode all over again.

He moved another domino into place, then sat back as Alex concentrated. Even after all this time, after fifteen years, he still missed her, still grieved. Still periodically took out all the information in the case file he'd kept active all these years because he refused to believe she was dead.

Gone, but not dead. He knew in his heart that his Rose had somehow managed to escape that watery grave and was somewhere else.

He supposed that made him a fanatic. Everyone else had accepted what they said was the inevitable. But he couldn't, wouldn't.

Maybe it was ridiculous, but he felt that if he did, then she really would be dead, that all chances of someday finding her would be erased.

He had to go on believing.

He had a wonderful family, children he loved, nephews and nieces he was proud of. Many men had less. A great deal less.

He wanted more.

He wanted Rose.

These days he waited until everyone had left for the precinct before he took out the file. He didn't want anyone pitying him or making any unwanted comments. He knew how much this bothered Rayne, who'd finally put it all behind her. He didn't want to jeopardize the progress she was making.

So he waited until they were all gone and the house was empty before going over the case again.

Except that these last few weeks, the house was never empty. Most of the time Ilene and the boy were here. But that was all right, too. It was good to have someone young around like Alex. It reminded him of better times, especially since the boy looked so much like his sons and nephews had when they were his age.

Alex moved another rectangle into place, then crowed as he held up his hands. All his game pieces were gone and there were none left to draw on. Andrew laughed, marveling at the sharpness of the boy's mind.

Dutifully, Andrew wrote down the number of pieces he still had in front of him. Alex had won three games in a row. When his kids were younger, in the rare instances that he was around to play with them, he'd always arranged it so they could win. He hadn't had to do that with Alex.

"Can we play another game?" Alex wanted to know.

He looked at his watch. "Okay, one more and then I have to start dinner."

"I'll help," Alex volunteered.

Andrew laughed. "You sure you're only four?"

"Five," Alex corrected mechanically as he began collecting the black rectangles and placing them face down on the table.

He stared at the boy, certain that he had misheard. "What?"

"Five," Alex repeated. He looked up before mixing up the dominos. "I'm not four, I'm five."

"Your mother says you're four."

The information made the boy pause, as if he was trying to reconcile it with what he knew to be true. And then he shrugged as he melded the pieces around one more time for luck. "Mama's sad. Maybe she forgot."

"Mothers don't forget something like that," Andrew assured him.

Alex began to count out his share of pieces.

"Then she made a mistake. I'm five." Pausing, he held up his right hand, using his fingers and thumb to illustrate. "See?"

"Yeah, I see," Andrew said slowly. And he did.

Tonight, after dinner, he was going to get back in the game again and do a little investigating of his own.

Chapter 14

Andrew closed the computer and leaned back. Around him the house was still. Everyone else had long since gone to sleep. Even Rayne. He'd heard her creeping in half an hour ago. It was close to one. He had no idea how the girl managed to keep going.

Batteries, probably.

He stared at the screen, thinking. He had his information. Looking up birth certificates was sinfully easy now when you knew what to do. He wasn't nearly as technologically naive as his children thought he was. It just served his purpose to pretend, get others to do his legwork. But he knew his way around the Internet better than any of them.

Alex O'Hara hadn't been born four years ago as Ilene had told them. The boy had been born five years ago. It was there, plain as day in the county records. She'd lied.

The only reason Andrew could come up with for Ilene's deception was that she didn't want Clay to know that he was the father. Which made Alex his grandson.

He smiled to himself. He'd had a feeling all along....

"We've got a grandson, Rose," he said softly to the eight-by-ten photograph that stood within a silver frame on his desk. "I know, I know, you're too young. So am I. But we'll get used to the idea."

His first instinct was to tell Clay, but that was the father in him talking. The detective within him advised caution and careful examination. There might be reasons he didn't know about. He needed to talk to Ilene first. Alone.

And that, he thought as he shut down the computer, was not going to be an easy matter. He was going to have to wait until everyone left in the morning.

From where he was standing the night seemed very long.

Clay had seemed antsy to her all last night, and it had only intensified this morning. Every time she asked him if there was anything wrong, he'd denied it, sometimes with a laugh, sometimes he would kiss her and they'd progress onto other things. Basically, he was shutting her out, she thought as she watched him from across the table. Maybe it was the beginning of the end. Again.

What else could it be?

Ilene picked at her toast, her appetite a no-show this morning. Maybe he was bracing himself to deliver the inevitable words: So long. She couldn't fool herself into thinking this was going to continue indefinitely, not with the indictment coming up tomorrow. Once that was behind them, things would all be out in the open. The news media would descend, and the D.A.'s office would do something formal for her and Alex's protection.

Which probably meant leaving here.

She didn't want to go.

Briefly she made eye contact with Clay, but then he looked away. Her heart began to sink. He was going to initiate another breakup. Things had been going too smoothly, which meant they were getting serious. He didn't like things to get too serious.

Last night the lovemaking had seemed a little off. Though he'd denied it, he'd been preoccupied, only half in the room. Was the other half getting ready to pack its bags and flee?

She watched him now as conversation flew around the breakfast table. He'd taken little part in any of it, allowing his siblings and the three cousins to dominate the table. He answered only when the occasional comment was directed his way.

And then, abruptly, he was getting up. Leaving. Something inside of her screamed *Mayday*.

"I've got to get going," he told his father, pushing his chair back under the table.

Busy serving up seconds to Shaw, Andrew nodded. "See you tonight."

Without waiting for an invitation she feared wouldn't come, Ilene rose to her feet, ready to walk him to the door. And to ask him one last time if there was anything wrong.

The way she knew there was.

She never got the chance.

He stopped short of the door, drawing her into the living room inside. "You know how you asked me earlier if there was something on my mind?"

Her heart had somehow crawled up in her throat, making breathing a real challenge. She felt as if everything she held dear was suddenly on the line. "Yes?"

"Well, there is."

Unconsciously squaring her shoulders, Ilene braced herself, ready for anything. Except for what she heard.

"Marry me."

For the first time in her life, her jaw dropped open, as if all the bones had suddenly been sucked out. "What?"

Clay held up two fingers. "Two words. First word, *marry,* rhymes with *carry.* Second word, *me,* rhymes with—"

There was this buzzing sound in her head, blotting

out his voice. She went on staring. "You're serious?"

"I never joke when I'm rhyming." Nerves danced wildly all through him. Clay had never thought he'd get the proposal, such as it was, out. Now that he finally had, this wasn't the way he'd hoped she would react. Like someone who found herself standing barefoot in a minefield. He went with the only conclusion he could. "You don't want to."

Like a woman possessed, she began to shake her head back and forth. "No, oh, God, no—"

Confusion intensified. Could he have been that wrong? He needed it spelled out. "'Oh God, no' as in, how could you think of asking me?"

Again she could only stare at him. How could he possibly even think that? "No, I want to marry you," she said quickly, "I've always wanted to marry you, but—why are you asking?"

It seemed rather a strange question, given that men had been proposing to women since they came out of the caves and donned shoes. "Because I decided to stop being a coward. And because I love you."

He loves me. The words echoed in her brain. He loved her. She was afraid to clutch them to her breast. "No other reason?"

He definitely was not following her thought process. "There's more?"

Her brain jumbled, she struggled to find the words

that would make him understand. "I mean, Alex doesn't have anything to do with it?"

So that was it. She was worried about how all this would affect her son. "Sure, Alex has something to do with it. I want him, too. I know the two of you are a package deal and—"

She couldn't bear to have him go down the wrong path. Ilene placed her finger to his lips, her heart hammering madly. Her moment of reckoning, she knew, had finally come. "I need to tell you something."

"Go ahead," he said warily.

"Alex isn't four, he's five." The sound of the back door opening and closing vaguely registered. Were people arriving or leaving? She wanted to flee with them. She took a deep breath. It didn't help. Ilene pushed on. "He's also yours."

"Why didn't you tell me?" His voice was deadly still, devoid of all emotion. She couldn't read the look in his eyes.

Words crashed together in her head. She had to make him understand. "I was the reason my parents got married. I was the reason life was a living hell for all of us. I wasn't going to let Alex go through that."

"Are you like your mother?"

"No."

He pinned her in place with a look that was darker than any she'd ever seen. "Am I like your father?"

"No."

"Well then?"

Her back to the wall, she fought back. This wasn't all on her. He deserved part of the blame.

"But you never once said you wanted to settle down, even someday. You thought marriage was okay for other people, but you made a point of letting me know that you weren't in that group." He began to say something, but she anticipated his protest. Clay probably thought she blamed him for that. "That's not to fault you, that's just dealing with what is."

He didn't know her, he thought. Not at all. Everything he'd thought he'd known, he didn't. She was a stranger. "If you'd only told me—"

"You would have done the honorable thing. Yes, I know." She closed her eyes to keep the tears from falling. She didn't even know if they were from anger or sorrow. Her eyes flew open again and she looked at him squarely, her hands clenched at her sides. "I didn't want the honorable thing. I wanted the I-can't-live-without-you-because-it-hurts-so-bad-it-rattles-my-teeth thing. There *is* no other reason to get married," she insisted. "Sometimes, that isn't enough, but it's a hell of a foundation, and without that, you've got nothing." She laughed shortly. "Believe me, I lived through it every day for eighteen years. I know. The second I turned eighteen, they got divorced and I left home."

The entire time they'd been together, she had barely mentioned her parents, but then, he hadn't really talked about his family, either. "I never knew."

She shrugged, dismissing the past. It did no good to dwell on it. Nothing could be changed.

"You never asked. You never wanted to know any real personal details about me," she reminded him. "Another hint that we weren't destined to experience the I-can't-live-without-you thing."

He had a son, a five-year-old son. And she hadn't told him. He felt as if someone had just kicked him in the gut. "I don't believe it."

She sighed. She supposed she should have seen this coming. It was a typical male reaction. "Alex is yours, there's never been anyone else."

"No, I'm not questioning that he's mine." She'd been a virgin when they'd first made love. "I just can't get past that you lied to me." Suddenly, a great deal of anger surged within him, anger he didn't know what to do with or how to channel. "I *asked* you if Alex was mine and you said no. You lied," he accused. "I would have bet the world would end before I would ever hear you utter a lie about anything."

There was no way to measure how awful, how guilty she felt. But it wasn't fair, she'd done it all for the best of reasons. To protect her son. "I'm sorry I'm not perfect."

He wanted to take her by her shoulders and shake her. She'd shattered his faith in her. She'd robbed him of something precious. "I didn't want you to be perfect, just honest.'' Suddenly he began backing away from her. He had to get away before things were said that couldn't be taken back. ''I'm sorry, but this is a little more than I can digest right now.''

Before she could say anything, he yanked open the front door and stormed out, feeling angrier than he could ever remember.

''I know where she's staying.''

Sitting at his desk, John Walken stiffened as the voice on the other end of the line finally said the words he'd been waiting to hear.

He didn't have to ask who it was. There was only one person on his mind these days, one person who stood between him and the resolution he'd been pinning all his hopes on.

''Well, don't just sit there talking to me, you know what you have to do,'' he snapped.

The woman had already proven that she was un-bribable. So it came down to this: Simplicity Computers was out of options. He was out of options. If the indictment was to go away, he needed to have Ilene O'Hara out of the picture. It wasn't something he relished having done, but there was no other way.

The other man replied with a graphic curse, then said, ''It's not that simple. She's staying with Andrew Cavanaugh.'' There was a pause, and when nothing was said, he added, ''The whole family's big in law enforcement.''

The smooth, unruffled manner he was known for

had completely deserted him. "So you make your move when the family's not around. They work, don't they?"

"Yes, but—"

"Good, do it then." He slammed down the receiver, breaking the connection.

Frowning, Walken took a few deep breaths, then looked at the painting he had on the wall. It was an original and had set him back a fortune. Ordinarily the colors soothed him.

But not today.

Life would have been a great deal better if he'd never hired that woman, he thought angrily. But her death wasn't going to be on his conscience. He'd given her a way out and she hadn't taken it.

This was on her head, not his.

"Everything all right?"

Caught off guard, Ilene swung around from the door that had just slammed. Clay's father stood behind her. There was sympathy in his eyes.

Tears threatened to fall from hers. With effort she raised her head, sealing her emotions inside.

"Just peachy," she answered. What was one more little lie in the face of the one she had committed herself to?

Andrew drew closer, his voice low. Understanding. "You told him?"

For the second time that morning, her mouth

dropped open. She'd been so careful. Or thought she'd been. "How did you…?"

"Alex told me." Seeing her bewildered look, he was quick to explain. "He said he was five, not four." His voice was kind, nonjudgmental, completely unlike his son's. "Birth certificates aren't all that hard to look up."

There was no use denying it. She felt like crumbling. Everywhere she looked, her life was caving in on her. "How long have you known?"

"Just since last night."

She thought of the scene she'd just gone through. "Why didn't you tell Clay?"

The look on Andrew's face told her that wasn't the way he operated. Above all else he was fair. And she hadn't been. "I wanted to talk to you first. Find out why you never said anything."

"Because I didn't want him marrying me for the wrong reasons."

"Love is never the wrong reason."

She looked at him. That had been the whole point. She didn't know if Clay loved her. "He never said anything about loving me."

He shook his head. There were times when, like George Bernard Shaw, his favorite playwright, he was utterly convinced that youth was wasted on the young. "Then take off your blinders, girl, because everything about that boy says he loves you. It's right out there for everyone to see."

If it was, she hadn't seen it. And she needed the words. "Well, not anymore. Not after this."

He knew Clay. Knew that his son had a tendency to blow up, then calm down again. To varying degrees, all his children did. They took after their mother that way. "Give him time, he'll come round." And then he smiled at her. "And thank you."

"Thank you?" she echoed, confused. "For what?"

He smiled warmly. "For giving me a wonderful grandson. He's a lot less of a handful than the five I got the first time around." He nodded toward the kitchen. "The others have gone. You want to sit and talk?"

"Not right now, but thank you," she added quickly. It meant so much to have him accept her this way. "I've got to go upstairs and see if Alex is awake yet." He'd woken up in the middle of the night, coughing and feeling generally miserable. A cold had materialized out of nowhere, and though she wasn't really concerned, she just wanted to dote on her son for a while and make him feel better.

He nodded. "I've already made up a tray for him. I can take it up if you want to be alone for a little while."

"No, that's all right. I'll bring it up to him. You've done more than enough for us already."

"It's not a matter of doing enough," he told her.

"It's a matter of family. Face it, you're part of ours now. No matter what."

She beamed with gratitude. She knew what he was saying. No matter what turn her relationship with Clay took.

The phone rang just then. Andrew glanced toward it. "Maybe that's Clay, ready to admit that he was a jackass and that he's sorry."

She laughed. "Don't count on it."

It wasn't Clay. She could tell by the look on Andrew's face after he said hello. Wanting to give him some privacy, she started to leave the room, but the look on the older man's face kept her from going.

"You sure?" he asked not once but twice. "All right, I'll be right down."

It was too early for the call to involve any of the people who had been here this morning. Still, she could see that whatever news he had received had completely unsettled Clay's father.

The moment he hung up, it was her turn to ask, "Are you all right?"

Numb, afraid to let his mind get carried away, he measured his words out slowly, as if he was debating drawing each one back in again.

"That was someone I used to work with. They found a homeless man dead in the park last night. He had one of those shopping carts next to him, filled with things he must have been collecting over the years." He shook his head. "Poor bastard." He'd come across scores of such twilight people during his years on the force, people so down on their luck they couldn't climb back up again, their minds backing away from reality. "They went through it, trying to see if they could find out who he was. My ex-partner said they found a beaten-up wallet on the bottom of the cart. It had my wife's driver's license in it."

That meant that somehow she'd gotten out. Rose wasn't lying in some watery grave all these years, she'd gotten out. He'd been right all along.

"So what are you waiting for?" she asked. "Go down to the precinct."

"Right." And then he stopped, the fog lifting from his brain. "I can't leave you alone."

She put her hand on his shoulder, turning him toward the door. "I am a big girl, Andrew. I can be left alone for a little while. Besides, no one's going to come," she assured him. There hadn't even been a mysterious phone call in the past two days. She was certain that Walken, if he was responsible for all this, had given up the futile attempts.

"If Alex is awake by now, he's probably bored out of his mind. I'll go upstairs and keep him company. I'm not you, of course, but in a pinch, his mom'll still do." She urged him toward the front door. "Go, find out what this is all about. Maybe it's the break you've been waiting for."

"Maybe," he agreed. Andrew took his jacket out of the hall closet and slipped it on. "I'll be back as soon as I can."

"I'll still be here." She thought of the scene between her and Clay. "At least for now."

Wanting to rush out, he still paused to reassure her. "You can stay for as long as you like."

That wouldn't be right. "This is Clay's house, I can't just—"

Andrew held up his hand, curtailing her flow of thought. "Clay moved out years ago. He came back because the guy he'd been subletting his apartment from wanted to move back in. We both knew it was only going to be for a little while, although our definitions of the word seem to differ.

"What I'm saying is that he could be out of here in a week. There's no reason for you to be leaving on his account. Besides, I still need to get better acquainted with my grandson."

Her protest was necessary, but only halfhearted. "But—"

"I don't want to hear another word about it," he told her with finality as he opened the front door. "Don't start giving me any grief, Ilene." He winked before leaving. "So far, that's what sets you apart from everyone else."

She took the tray that Andrew had fixed to her son and watched him eat. There was nothing wrong with the boy's appetite, which was a good sign. As she took the tray away and set it off to the side, she peered at his face. His eyes didn't look a hundred percent well.

She touched her lips to his forehead. It was cool, but that didn't immediately mean he was better. "Still feel icky?"

Alex nodded, then looked at her hopefully. "Andrew said he was going to bring me some ice cream to make my throat feel better."

This after a mountain of pancakes. She shook her head. "That's only when they take your tonsils out."

She watched his small eyebrows pull together in consternation. "Do I have those?"

"Yes."

The hopeful look made a reappearance. "Can we take them out?"

She laughed. "Not today. I'll see about some ice cream later," she promised, when he looked dejected. There wasn't much she'd deny him. Fortunately for both of them, she thought, Alex reacted well to being spoiled. There wasn't a bratty, demanding bone in his body. "Right now why don't we see if *The Cat in the Hat* wants to come out and play?"

Reaching for the book, she thought she heard a car pulling up. Andrew hadn't been gone all that long. She was certain he couldn't have gotten the information he wanted so quickly.

Clay, maybe it was Clay.

She called herself an idiot when her heart began to pound. "Listen, I think I hear someone coming." She saw the eager look on her son's face and guessed what he was thinking. "Oh no, you stay here young man. I'll go see who it is."

Making him promise to remain in his room, she closed Alex's door and all but flew down the stairs. Praying all the while. As she got to the foyer she heard the doorknob being turned. Reaching for it, she yanked the door open, ready to throw herself into Clay's arms.

"Forget your key?"

Her wide smile froze. It wasn't Clay. The man on the doorstep was tall and muscular. His eyes were flat. She'd never seen him before.

"I never had one."

Chapter 15

The next moment the man began to force his way in. Ilene grabbed hold of the door with both hands and tried to slam it shut in his face.

The effort was futile. She was far from a weakling but he had height and girth on his side. Using his shoulder, he shoved his way into the house as if she were no more of a deterrent than a flea.

Her eyes never leaving his face, she backed away. When she saw the opened telephone book someone in the house had left out, she heaved it at him. He ducked in time. She began grabbing and throwing anything she could get her hands on.

The intruder blocked every throw with his arm, and all the while he kept relentlessly coming at her. A sense of panic mounted in her chest.

Where had he come from? Had he been watching the house all along? "What do you want from me?"

"It's not what I want. I'm just the messenger." His voice was low, unflappable. "And you know what this is about. Don't make this any more difficult than it already is, Ilene," he taunted her. "You don't want this to be painful."

"Just final, right?" She struggled to keep her voice from cracking. "Someone'll be back any minute." She knew they wouldn't be, but hoped *he* didn't. "You're not going to get away with this."

There was mild amusement on his face as he watched her get behind the sofa, placing it between them. "You'd be surprised at what I've gotten away with over the years. And in a few minutes none of this is going to matter to you anymore."

"Mama?" Her eyes darted toward the top of the stairs. Alex wasn't there, but in another moment he would be. Panic spiked up high within her. She saw the man looking toward the stairs.

"Stay where you are, Alex," she called.

And then, to her horror, she saw the man turn from her and head toward the stairs. Adrenaline flowed through every part of her body. He was going to hurt her son. She couldn't let that happen.

"No!"

With a wild cry, she threw herself at the man, managing to tackle him. He crashed to the floor at the foot of the stairs.

Caught completely off guard, he'd been able to

offer little resistance. He went down, hitting his head against the bottom step.

It was enough only to daze him for a split second. His face contorted as he cursed loudly at her. She tried to move out of his way, but he grabbed her. His large hands went around her throat.

She knew he was going to kill her.

Struggling, she managed to bring her knee up and make solid contact with his groin. The blow made him wither long enough for her to scramble away.

Enraged, he grabbed her leg and dragged her back down. She hit her head.

Everything started to spin.

She felt his hands go around her throat again. This time his body pinned her down, completely immobilizing her.

Ilene tried to scream. Nothing came out. There was no air.

No air.

Desperately trying to hang on to consciousness, she still felt it slipping through her fingers.

Who was going to take care of Alex?

And Clay...

Clay...

A darkness closed in around her, taking with it all thoughts, all surroundings.

Everything.

Leaving only blackness in its place.

And then there was noise, a distant, faraway

noise. Like someone shouting. But she couldn't grasp hold. She was too weak.

And then there was a louder noise, like thunder cracking. The weight on her chest grew intolerable, pressing her down. Crushing her.

Then there was nothing.

She was dead.

But if this was heaven, it was awfully noisy. And rough. Something, some*one* was handling her, pushing on her body. No, on her chest.

One, two, three…

Air, there was air. Air was being blown into her mouth. Minty air.

She started to choke, to cough. To gasp. Air…she needed more air.

Her eyes flying open, she sucked it in, grasping huge chunks and feeding off them. Until the darkness began to abate.

It was several seconds before she realized that she was looking up at Clay.

Clay.

Relief flooded through her, washing away the fear. She sat bolt upright, throwing her arms around his neck and sobbing his name.

He was afraid to release the emotions churning so violently inside of him, afraid that if he did, he was going to break down so badly, he might never be able to pull any of the pieces together again. She'd been so still when he'd administered CPR it had scared the hell out of him.

And now he couldn't say anything, couldn't think. So he said nothing, only held her close to him, stroking her hair and thanking God that he wasn't as pigheaded as he'd once been. That he had given in to a sense stronger than his pride and returned to try to sort things out with Ilene.

If he hadn't, there would never have been anything more to sort out. She would have been—

He wouldn't let his mind go there.

When he could finally trust his voice, he asked softly, "Are you all right?"

She raised her head from his shoulder and weakly nodded. "Yes." The word crawled slowly up her constricted throat.

The man he'd shot had been so strong looking, Clay had been afraid he was going to break her neck. He raised her head slightly to examine her throat. "You're going to have bruises."

She took a deep breath. It was a little easier this time.

"But I'll live to see them." She looked over toward the slumped form of the man who had just tried to kill her. He wasn't moving. "Is he dead?"

Reluctantly Clay shifted away from her and felt the man's pulse. It was reedy, but it was still steady. "No. Just knocked out."

There was no question in his mind that if the hired killer had carried out his agenda, he would never have left alive. This would have been one matter he wouldn't have left to the courts.

Rising to his feet, he took out his cell phone and punched in a code. The moment he heard the line being picked up, he quickly recited the particulars that would get them immediate special assistance.

"Mama?"

By the time she looked, Alex had made it to the bottom of the stairs, his small face a mask of fear. Drawn by the noise and the raised voices, he'd finally ventured out of his room. He flung himself into her arms, clearly frightened.

She struggled not to cry. Tears would only frighten the boy more. So she summoned the steadiest voice she could, under the circumstances, and stroked his head as she held him to her. "It's okay, baby, it's okay. Nobody's going to hurt you."

Pulling back, he looked at her with his huge, inquisitive eyes. "You, Mama, are they going to hurt you?"

Her heart swelled as she drew her son to her again, holding him against her chest. He was so old for his tender years. But it was Clay who addressed the boy's concern and answered his question.

"No, Alex, nobody's going to hurt you or your mother ever again." Sirens heralded the ambulance's approach, as well as the squad car that was following in its wake. Clay looked around. "Where's my father?" he asked suddenly. He realized that he hadn't seen the car in the driveway. At the time, the flung-open door had stolen all of his attention.

Her head still swimming, she struggled to remember. "He got a call from an ex-partner. Something about finding your mother's wallet." She looked at the man who was beginning to come to. "I guess he must have been watching the house."

"Or had someone place the call." Which meant that a great deal of work had been put into not only learning where Ilene had been taken, but into finding out everything about the people who had taken her in. His first thought was that there was a mole somewhere in the department. Very few people outside the family actually knew where she was staying.

She hadn't thought of that, hadn't thought of anything except protecting her son. But now that Clay had brought the matter up, the idea chilled her down to the bone. It made Walken seem like a monster who didn't care what kind of consequences his actions had. "That's terrible."

"Not as terrible as things might have been," he said significantly.

The next moment the house was filled with paramedics and police personnel, not to mention Santini, who had caught Clay's call into the department on the police scanner.

Circumventing the man on the floor, he crossed to Ilene and her son. "Everybody all right here?"

Taking Clay's hand, the other lightly braced on Alex's shoulder so he wouldn't feel slighted, Ilene got to her feet. The room swayed a little, and she held on to Clay's hand more tightly than she'd intended. She saw the concern in his eyes.

"We're fine." She deliberately looked at Clay. "Now."

"You're still going to the hospital." Clay beckoned to one of the paramedics. "I want you thoroughly checked out."

She began to protest, though there wasn't much feeling behind the words. Her energy level still hadn't returned.

Santini edged over to her side. "Better listen to him."

She smiled. "Do I have a choice?"

Clay's partner winked at her. "He always gets his vehicles thoroughly checked out before he commits to them."

Puzzled, she looked from one man to another. "What's that supposed to mean?"

"It means that Santini's got entirely too much time on his hands." Clay looked down at Alex. It was the first time he'd seen the boy since he'd found out that he was his father. He felt something strange going on inside of him. The lid on his emotions threatened to blow sky-high any second. "You ever ride in an ambulance before?" Alex shook his head. "If you're real good, maybe we can get them to let you sound the siren."

Alex looked very serious. Behind him, the paramedics were strapping his mother's potential killer onto a gurney. "Will they take care of Mama?"

Clay moved out of the way as the paramedics guided the gurney out to the ambulance. Here he was, trying to distract him, and all Alex could think of was his mother's welfare. He was bowled over by the boy's maturity. "Yes."

Alex nodded solemnly. "Okay."

Unable to resist, Santini ruffled Alex's hair. "Great kid you got there." It wasn't entirely clear whether he was addressing Ilene exclusively or not.

The first paramedic went to Ilene. "Can you walk?"

"My head's a little fuzzy and I'll probably have to forget about a professional singing career," she cracked, running her hand along her throat, "but there's nothing wrong with my legs."

"If you'll follow me," the man requested, "we'll see about getting you to the hospital."

But as the man began to take Ilene to the back of the opened vehicle, Clay put up his hand. He nodded at the man he'd wounded, the man he still wanted to kill with his bare hands. They'd loaded him on first. "She doesn't ride with him."

The man didn't frighten her any longer. She had Clay. Ilene placed her hand on his arm, drawing his attention. "It's all right."

No, Clay thought, it wasn't. The bastard had tried to kill her, he wasn't about to put her through having to share space with him. Clay looked at the paramedic. "I called in for two wagons."

About to answer him, the attendant was relieved

to hear the sound of a second ambulance approaching. "And there it is now." He smiled at Ilene, obviously happy to withdraw. "They'll take good care of you."

With that, he climbed into the rear of the vehicle and pulled the doors closed behind him.

Right outside the E.R. exam room the halls were littered with Cavanaughs. Almost all of them had poked their heads in at one point or another while Ilene waited to be ministered to by the doctor and hopefully released. Andrew had been almost the first on the scene and he had taken Alex under his wing after first expressing his profound apologies for ever having left her.

She'd absolved him of any responsibility three times over before he'd finally retreated with her son. His grandson.

They made a nice pair, she'd thought. All in all, it had turned out alright. Her son now had the grandfather she'd always wanted him to have. An attentive one who cared about him.

The man who had come to kill her was going to live. Not only that, but according to Santini, once he'd come to, he seemed more than willing to name names in exchange for special consideration. The first name he'd given them was Walken's.

There was no need for her to remain in hiding any longer. The way things were going, she would be able to reclaim a normal life very, very soon.

But she wasn't thinking about that now. All of her attention was fixed on the man who had refused, even after the E.R. doctor had strongly recommended it, to leave her side. He'd stood by her, holding her hand all through the exam, asking more questions than she would have ever thought to ask.

Sitting down on the edge of the bed, he took her hand in his. He knew he had to talk fast. The doctor might return any second to release her and then she'd be engulfed by the mob that had collected outside the door. He needed to get this out before then.

"Why did you come back?" Ilene asked.

"Because I remembered that the last thing that happened between my parents was an argument. I've seen the toll it's taken on my father and I don't want that happening to us." And then he smiled as he finally allowed relief to flood through his veins. She was going to be all right. And for as long as fate allowed, she was going to be his. He was determined about that. "Besides, I thought I could talk you into accepting my proposal by using my charm."

He still wanted to marry her. Despite the deception. She looked into his eyes and knew that he loved her. Really loved her. It was all that mattered. She blinked, in vain trying to keep back the tears that were suddenly gathering. "Yes."

About to launch into a whole list of reasons why she should marry him, Clay stopped abruptly. "Yes?" he echoed uncertainly.

Her smile spread to every part of her. If she had

ever felt any happier, Ilene couldn't remember when. "Yes."

He feigned a dubious look. "But I haven't even turned on my charm yet."

Lord, but she loved this man. Sometimes, she thought, happy endings did happen. And this was hers. "Heroes turn me on."

"Heroes," he echoed, as if mulling the concept over. "Does this mean I'm going to have to go out and slay a dragon every so often?"

Amusement danced in her eyes. "Or at the very least a lizard."

"But I like lizards," he protested. "So does Alex." He'd found that out about the boy. Something else they had in common. Each day with them under his father's roof had proved to be a revelation.

Clay had no idea how he'd managed to get so damn lucky. He'd blown it all those years ago, and now he was getting a second chance to make things right. Permanently.

"Okay," she said, surrendering, "don't slay it, just capture it." And then the humor left her eyes. She should have told him about Alex a long time ago. Maybe all of this would have been spared them. And Alex would have had a real father these five years.

As if reading her expression, he took her into his arms.

The last brick in the wall that had surrounded her

heart broke in two. "Oh, God, Clay, I've been such an idiot."

He kissed her hair, breathing in the scent. So grateful to be able to hold her like this. He could have lost her today. Forever. And so many things would have been left unsaid. "Yeah, me, too."

She sniffed, trying to hold back the tears. Not doing a very good job of it. "How is it our son turned out so well?"

He felt her words warm against his shoulder as she spoke. The warmth spread, filling his heart. He held her closer. "Must be recessive genes."

Ilene drew her head back to look at him. "I love you, Clay Cavanaugh. I always have."

He knew that. It no longer frightened him. Now it was his strength. "The feeling is mutual." Then, because the words couldn't be kept back any longer, he said, "I love you."

"Then why didn't you ever say anything?"

He shrugged, giving her the only explanation that seemed plausible right now. "That idiot thing we were just talking about." And then he smiled. "But don't worry. I've got the rest of my life to make up for it."

"I'm not worried."

It was the last thing she said before he kissed her.

Epilogue

It was late.

Andrew switched on the light in his den and closed the door behind him. Everyone had finally settled in. After they'd brought Ilene and Alex back with them, Clay had gathered everyone at the house and made the announcement. He'd told them all that Alex was his son. And that soon Ilene would be his wife.

A lot of joy today, Andrew thought, smiling. There'd been a lot to celebrate, and if there was one thing the Cavanaughs knew how to do, it was celebrate. The last of them had finally cleared out at eleven.

The house was quiet now.

Andrew sat down at his desk. The desk where

he'd spent hours at a time poring over his notes, trying to find one shred of evidence, one fact, however slim, that he could use to support what he always believed in his heart to be true. That Rose was alive.

He had it now.

Here, carefully wrapped in a plastic bag, tagged as evidence but important to no one but him, he had proof. Proof that she hadn't been trapped in her car when it sank to the bottom of its watery grave. Proof that she'd managed to get out on her own, that she hadn't been swept away by the current.

He placed in on his desk and looked through the plastic at the worn, cracked leather. He'd given this to Rose, filled with the pictures of their children. The pictures were still there. As was her license.

He'd kept the news of this discovery to himself, at least for now. He hadn't wanted to spoil Clay's news tonight, hadn't wanted to cast a shadow on the party that followed.

He knew what they all thought, that he'd become obsessed with this, with finding Rose. But it wasn't an obsession, it was a belief, a very firm belief. If Rose had been dead, something inside of him would have been, too, something would have shattered.

But it hadn't, it wasn't.

He was intact. The emptiness that was there was because he missed her, not because he grieved over her lost life.

If she was dead, he would know.

''You've got a lot to live for, Rose. Now more than ever. And I'm going to bring you home,'' he promised the woman in the photograph.

Quietly he set the frame down again. Rising, Andrew placed the wrapped wallet back in his pocket, then turned off the light.

Before going up the stairs, he checked the front porch light, making sure it was on, just the way he did every night.

The light was left on to guide Rose up the steps in case she came home tonight.

* * * * *

If you liked CRIME AND PASSION, you'll love Marie Ferrarella's next CAVANAUGH JUSTICE romance, DANGEROUS GAMES, coming to you from Intimate Moments in early February 2004. Don't miss it!

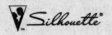

Your opinion is important to us! Please take a few moments to share your thoughts with us about your experiences with Harlequin and Silhouette books. Your comments will be very useful in ensuring that we deliver books you love to read. *Please take a few minutes to complete the questionnaire, then send it to us at the address below.*

Send your completed questionnaires to:
Harlequin/Silhouette Reader Survey, P.O. Box 9046, Buffalo, NY 14269-9046

1. As you may know, there are many different lines under the Harlequin and Silhouette brands. Each of the lines is listed below. Please check the box that most represents your reading habit for each line.

Line	Currently read this line	Do not read this line	Not sure if I read this line
Harlequin American Romance	❑	❑	❑
Harlequin Duets	❑	❑	❑
Harlequin Romance	❑	❑	❑
Harlequin Historicals	❑	❑	❑
Harlequin Superromance	❑	❑	❑
Harlequin Intrigue	❑	❑	❑
Harlequin Presents	❑	❑	❑
Harlequin Temptation	❑	❑	❑
Harlequin Blaze	❑	❑	❑
Silhouette Special Edition	❑	❑	❑
Silhouette Romance	❑	❑	❑
Silhouette Intimate Moments	❑	❑	❑
Silhouette Desire	❑	❑	❑

2. Which of the following best describes why you bought *this book?* One answer only, please.

the picture on the cover	❑	the title	❑
the author	❑	the line is one I read often	❑
part of a miniseries	❑	saw an ad in another book	❑
saw an ad in a magazine/newsletter	❑	a friend told me about it	❑
I borrowed/was given this book	❑	other: _____	❑

3. Where did you buy *this book?* One answer only, please.

at Barnes & Noble	❑	at a grocery store	❑
at Waldenbooks	❑	at a drugstore	❑
at Borders	❑	on eHarlequin.com Web site	❑
at another bookstore	❑	from another Web site	❑
at Wal-Mart	❑	Harlequin/Silhouette Reader	
at Target	❑	Service/through the mail	❑
at Kmart	❑	used books from anywhere	❑
at another department store or mass merchandiser	❑	I borrowed/was given this book	❑

4. On average, how many Harlequin and Silhouette books do you buy at one time?

I buy _____ books at one time	❑
I rarely buy a book	❑

MRQ403SIM-1A

5. How many times per month do you shop for any *Harlequin and/or Silhouette* books?
One answer only, please.

1 or more times a week	❏	a few times per year	❏
1 to 3 times per month	❏	less often than once a year	❏
1 to 2 times every 3 months	❏	never	❏

6. When you think of your ideal heroine, which *one* statement describes her the best?
One answer only, please.

She's a woman who is strong-willed	❏	She's a desirable woman	❏
She's a woman who is needed by others	❏	She's a powerful woman	❏
She's a woman who is taken care of	❏	She's a passionate woman	❏
She's an adventurous woman	❏	She's a sensitive woman	❏

7. The following statements describe types or genres of books that you may be
interested in reading. Pick *up to 2 types* of books that you are most interested in.

I like to read about truly romantic relationships	❏
I like to read stories that are sexy romances	❏
I like to read romantic comedies	❏
I like to read a romantic mystery/suspense	❏
I like to read about romantic adventures	❏
I like to read romance stories that involve family	❏
I like to read about a romance in times or places that I have never seen	❏
Other: _____	❏

*The following questions help us to group your answers with those readers who are
similar to you. Your answers will remain confidential.*

8. Please record your year of birth below.
19 ____

9. What is your marital status?

| single | ❏ | married | ❏ | common-law | ❏ | widowed | ❏ |
| divorced/separated | ❏ |

10. Do you have children 18 years of age or younger currently living at home?
yes ❏   no ❏

11. Which of the following best describes your employment status?

| employed full-time or part-time | ❏ | homemaker | ❏ | student | ❏ |
| retired | ❏ | unemployed | ❏ |

12. Do you have access to the Internet from either home or work?
yes ❏   no ❏

13. Have you ever visited eHarlequin.com?
yes ❏   no ❏

14. What state do you live in?
_____

15. Are you a member of Harlequin/Silhouette Reader Service?
yes ❏   Account # _____   no ❏   MRQ403SIM-1B

If you enjoyed what you just read,
then we've got an offer you can't resist!

Take 2 bestselling
love stories FREE!
Plus get a FREE surprise gift!

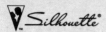

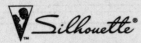
Silhouette®

COMING NEXT MONTH

SIMCNM1103